#1 SILVER CREEK RANCH:
FORGOTTEN

#1 SILVER CREEK RANCH: FORGOTTEN

Claudia Monteiro

iUniverse, Inc.
Bloomington

#1 Silver Creek Ranch
Forgotten

iUniverse books may be ordered through booksellers or by contacting:

iUniverse
1663 Liberty Drive
Bloomington, IN 47403
www.iuniverse.com
1-800-Authors (1-800-288-4677)

Because of the dynamic nature of the Internet, any web addresses or links contained in this book may have changed since publication and may no longer be valid. The views expressed in this work are solely those of the author and do not necessarily reflect the views of the publisher, and the publisher hereby disclaims any responsibility for them.

ISBN: 978-1-4502-6075-6 (sc)
ISBN: 978-1-4502-6076-3 (ebk)

Printed in the United States of America

iUniverse rev. date: 09/23/2010

With boundless time his hooves strike earth

And with his freedom comes rebirth

His liberty manifests to such great distance

He races wind with no resistance

His eyes blaze wild with fired pride

A summoned spirit with every stride

Majestic heart, a beating song

Unbroken rhythm forever on

He'd jump the mountains and face a storm

Not just strong or fast, or bold...but warm

His beauty given by a glorious source

He be but only the impeccable Horse!

~Claudia Monteiro~

CHAPTER 1

Callie Marshall sat in sixth period, eager for class to end. If she had to listen to Mr. Fareweather lecture one more word about the importance of MLA format for their essays due in a few days, her head was sure to explode. Five more minutes to endure and she could go home and take her beautiful, dark, blood bay mare, Romana, out for a nice long trail ride before she even considered homework.

"Again," droned Mr. Fareweather, "Make sure to structure out an introductory paragraph, then include your body paragraphs and then a closing paragraph to summarize all of your points. Watch out for..."

She stuck his monotone voice in the background where she thought it belonged and insightfully planned out the rest of her day.

First, she would go home and help her father feed the horses. Her dad, David Cristofer Marshall, was a well-known and respected horse rancher around here. Her mother, Lilly Deveron Marshall, stayed at home, helping take care of the ranch life with her husband. She managed the financial side of business. The Marshalls owned myriads of cattle, but they also offered the extra service of Fishing and Guiding on their property for earning extra money to support the ranch. People loved to venture on their land and accompanying her mother on tours that offered learning about the areas and places great for visiting. As well, during the summer, Silver Creek offered people to come and fish, hunt and camp for a specified time.

Ten horses to feed and ten stalls to muck out and lay fresh bedding for. But Noah Thomas Riley, one of their two ranch hands, was always around to help Callie out with barn chores.

Callie really liked Noah. And not just in the friendly way. She was seventeen - finishing high school - and he was twenty. Her birthday would be coming soon enough, though, and she hoped that Noah liked her back in the same way.

She smiled to herself as she pictured him in dark blue jeans, sturdy boots, handsome t-shirt, and his attractive black Stetson sitting on his short, cropped black hair, his sweet deep hazel eyes and his perfectly tanned russet skin. He was almost six feet tall and was lean, fit and broad from the constant work he performed at the ranch.

Callie shook her head and tried to focus again.

After the horses were taken care of she would saddle up Romana and escape for a good hour or two. Coming back, she would grudgingly face homework right after dinner.

The bell rang and grasped back her attention to the present. She slammed her books shut and quickly shoved them in her knapsack, shot up from her chair and flew out the door in an excited rush. Callie maneuvered herself through the mobs and clusters of students and finally reached her locker.

Romana, she was certain, would be anxiously waiting for a good gallop through Silver Creek Ranch.

Unlike everyone else in her family, Callie rode her mare in English equipment, but Romana was also occasionally ridden in a western saddle, too. Most of Silver Creek's horses were considered superb reining and cutting horses.

Callie was known as the "English Cowgirl" because she tended to ride in an English saddle, with pasture boots and half chaps, along with her Stetson cowgirl hats.

But her father also called her his "Callie Bear" which Noah would tease her about playfully on regular intervals. She didn't mind.

As she tucked the rest of her school books into her pack, she remembered her mom was out of town dealing with financial matters and running errands, so she would have to fix dinner herself and her dad. Maybe even bake her famous chocolate chip cookies and make home-made ice cream so they could have ice cream sandwiches for dessert like her dad very much enjoyed. Callie figured it would be a delightful treat for her hard working ranch family; she'd even save some for her mom.

Once she closed her locker and heard the device click securely in place, she slung her backpack on her shoulder and half ran to catch her bus.

"Callie, wait up a minute!" called Andrew down the hall. He jogged to catch up to her.

Callie made a face before whirling around and faked a smile. She attempted an excuse to get rid of him.

"Hi Andrew, I really can't take right now, I have to catch my bus." She really didn't like him.

Sure, he acted nice around her -for show- but Andrew Dale, in her point of view, was a stuck-up, egotistical jock who was a constant hassle. She wasn't positive as to why he had built such a liking to her, but she suspected he was looking for more than friendship.

He scratched his short, dirty blond hair and frowned at the hasty dismissal but shrugged it off otherwise. The rejection didn't touch his plain brown eyes. Instead, determination filled them. He wasn't one to give in so easily.

"Well, okay. Maybe some other time, then?" he tried, hoping to trap her in a promise he knew she'd feel obligated to keep.

"Er... Sure. See you around, Andrew. Bye!"

Callie scurried out the double doors of Powder River High School before he thought of something to stall her, and caught her bus as it prepped to leave.

Taking her seat, she glanced out the window and let her mind wander.

She never did have many friends, but she did have one. Callie held sight of Angela Raymond and motioned her cheerful best friend to come and sit next to her.

Angela's dark, red streaked, brown hair ran to the small of her back, falling neatly behind her shoulders as she gladly offered Callie a glowing grin and came to join her. Freckles dotted her rosy, tanned cheeks and face.

"Hey, Callie, what's up girl?" she asked brightly.

Callie returned the smile. "Same old, same old," she replied.

The bus returned its routinely drop offs down the town and country roads of Natrona County, Wyoming. Callie's ranch was located north of the town of Powder River and Yellowstone Highway. The bus accessed it by travelling north on County Road 106. She loved living in Equality State and absorbing the scenic byways of her wild and productive country. It was like looking at astounding 360 panoramic views.

The girls perpetually continued talking and gushing about their day.

"I thought the bell would never free us of class. Mr. Fareweather's essay lecture was driving me crazy!" said Callie.

"Tell me about it!" exclaimed Angela.

Callie felt really glad she could have such an extraordinary best friend to talk to. It caused the thought of her not having many friends seem less important. Angela's good moods were infectious.

She could never help feeling pleasantly cheerful

whenever she hung around Angela. It was contagious. She never acted around anyone. Never wore a false mask. She was truthful and trustworthy, and interested in how Callie actually felt and shared her enthusiasm.

"Are you going for a ride later?" asked Angela. "I bet Romana is dying for a good run!"

"Of course!" Callie chimed ecstatically.

Angela usually rode on Tuesdays with Callie. However, today her friend notified her in first period that she couldn't make it on account of a dentist appointment. She had begged her mom to reschedule, but she might as well have been trying to make a wall move for all the good it did her. Her mother wouldn't budge.

The girls would just have to wait till next week.

When Callie rode Romana -of course- Angela always preferred sweet, calm, tempered Daisy.

Ironically enough, Daisy and Romana were best friends just like Angela and Callie.

Soon enough, the bus hit Callie's stop and broke an end to their threading conversation. She erected herself and waved to her best friend goodbye.

"See you tomorrow, Angie!" she bellowed.

"You bet!" Angie hollered back enthusiastically.

The bus wheeled away, creating plumes of dust clouds that settled calmly back to the ground as Callie walked the rest of the way home. Once she covered the small remaining distance, the wooden intricate plaque labeled "Silver Creek Ranch" came into view. That's when fencing from the property's pasture started stretching out in front of her.

She quickened her pace at the sense of untamable energy.

Like always, the dark, blood bay mare waited for Callie far out in the field. When her horse caught a glimpse of her best companion, she rapturously trotted down the hill in her direction.

Strong drifting hooves grated the earth below her and her coal black mane flickered amid her neck. Her nostrils flared, testing the light breeze and drawing in Callie's scent as her human leapt over the fence.

The two met with one another in this spot every day after school and Callie would ride her majestic mare bareback and bridleless down to the barn. With all of her ceaseless physical activity, she was considered as fit as a fiddle; a restless spirit always on the move.

Romana happily approached with her ears perked forward. Callie stood still and reached out her hand so that her horse would touch her first. She never forced, but rather always asked permission, because there could always be days that Romana never felt like being ridden. When she didn't, she was always content enough to walk along side her and play with her a little.

Her mount's velvety muzzle made contact with her hand and she tenderly rubbed it, moving up towards her neck and smoothly came to stand next to her withers, scratching them affectionately. She then adjusted the loose hanging strap from her bag onto her other shoulder so her baggage would sit squarely and climbed aboard the patient mare's back. Hugging her legs around the barrel, Callie clutched two handfuls of soft mane and only needed to squeeze her legs with an ounce of pressure. Romana needed no further instruction and sauntered forward to home at complete liberty.

As Callie rode, she could see in the distance Bighorn Mountains. It was on the northwest part of the ranch and could be reached by the Red Wall Country Byway; an unpaved road with magnificent natural scenery with a pioneer history. But it also traversed though the historic ghost town of Arminto and its Stock Trail and Buffalo Creek Road which was still presently in use for cattle drives.

Half way down the vast stretch of open field, Callie's two best buddies appeared uncontainably wagging their tails till they looked like they would fall right off. The two Labrador retrievers came to greet Callie and welcome her home like they always did on a daily basis after school.

"Bailey! Panther!" she addressed the chocolate retriever and the black retriever. "My two best boys! Race ya' home?"

She was already shifting Romana into a new gear and the dogs didn't need any more than that. They turned and ran.

This was second nature for Callie to be on a horse. She grew up on horses' backs. All her life there was no way to untether her bond to them. No way at all. It felt ever so free to race the challenging wind and outrun the speedy dogs.

Romana hated losing, so she picked up her velocity, her sheer Quarter horse kicking in, and Callie did nothing but pretend to physically morph with her horse and move as if they were one instead of two.

Bailey and Panther had been fast, but not fast enough for the steadfast Thoroughbred Quarter horse.

Callie slipped off her back and climbed over the fence to the other side, giving Romana a face cradling kiss before she parted and the dogs followed behind her up to the house.

When Callie trudged into the barn in a change of comfortable barn clothes and had her long, light brown hair in a neat braid, she examined the work that needed her attention.

Nine various colored horse heads curiously peered out at her and synchronizingly said hello with neighs and whinnies. From down the aisle, Adrian appeared and waved.

"The horses have all been fed," he informed. "Except for Romana," he laughed. "That silly mare of yours always insists on carrying you the rest of the way home before taking one bite of her feed." He shook his head with a friendly, teasing smile that illustrated his fondness of Callie and her relationship with horses. "Same goes for your wagging troublemakers there," he gestured at Bailey and Panther, amused.

"You know how they are," said Callie. "Wouldn't expect anything less than a welcome home party," she chuckled, patting one of the dogs.

Adrian Farren was their other ranch hand, and a great family friend. He and her father were almost like brothers.

The 31-year old wiped his forehead with the back of his hand and swept his fingers through his brown unkempt hair. His pale, murky blue eyes fixed on her emerald greens with luminous yellow rings in the irises.

"Before I forget, your father and I have to run out an errand. We should be back within an hour or two. I was hoping you and Noah could muck the stalls. And your father wanted me to ask you a favor for him."

"Sure. What do you need?"

Just as he opened his mouth and was about to request the service needed, Noah strode in with a grin on his face the second he saw Callie standing in the middle of the aisle way.

"Hey, Cowgirl!"

"Hey, Noah!"

"Have a good day at school?" he asked.

It brightened Callie's mood by a significant contrast whenever he asked her that. Everyday he asked her how her day was. But she hoped he was interested in more than just her school affairs.

"Sure," Callie lied.

Noah knew her better. "That boring, huh?"

It always surprised her how well he seemed to know her. He read her like a book. It shouldn't have of course, but Callie had known Noah as long as three years when her father first hired him.

David never regretted it, either. Noah was a hard worker and a fine, exceptional hand; he never failed to go beyond the call of duty and what was expected of him.

"Yes, very boring," she confirmed, unashamed.

Noah laughed at her response.

She didn't have anything against school, but when she lived on a 92, 200 acre ranch with ten horses to spend the day with, it was very simple to lose her concentration and count down the minutes till it was over. Her attention span would lapse and the only productive brain activity she allowed was daydreaming about horses.

Callie was extremely lucky and fortunate to have two loving and caring parents who shared her love of horses and were very well known horse people.

Before the mild greeting transformed into a blabbering conversation, Adrian backtracked himself to his question before he was interrupted.

"Noah good thing you're here." He turned to Callie. "Your father needs you two to head into town and pick up some supplies."

Callie and Noah exchanged glances. She wanted to make an objection but quickly gave it a second thought; Romana would just have to wait.

"Of course," said Noah. "What supplies do you need?"

Adrian fished out a folded and creased piece of paper with a point form list of necessities scrawled on it.

Noah reached out and took the list, transferring it into his own jean pocket. "Consider it done."

"Great," said Adrian. "Thanks."

Callie sighed, disappointed.

A horn from her father's pick up truck honked and that was Dad signaling for Adrian to get a move on. Callie followed behind and hurriedly waved to her dad, blowing a kiss in his direction. Adrian plopped on the passenger's seat and closed the door. Rolling down the window, David Marshall gave his daughter a wink. "I'll be home soon, Callie Bear!" he called. Callie only nodded and waved till the truck vanished in the flurry of dust resulted from the tires.

Returning to the barn, Noah had already rummaged out the wheelbarrows. His lips curved, revealing gleaming white teeth against his moderately sable skin.

"Nothing like mucking out stalls," he chuckled, handing her a pitchfork.

Callie giggled, amused. "Beats sitting in class all day long," she pointed out.

Noah couldn't argue with that.

He worked away on five of the ten horse stalls -Star, Denver, Bandit, Trigger, and his own horse, Black Bear. Bear was Noah's proud Quarter Horse gelding whose coat beamed a brilliant coal black with no markings of any sort. The horse could travel through the night completely unnoticed. He could blend in with the darkness, unseen.

Meanwhile, Callie labored away on the other five including her own mare -Romana, Bliss, Daisy, Pretty Lady (Lady), and Mocha.

She wondered if Noah would give her an opinion on what she should make for dinner. Adrian and Noah frequently stayed to eat with them. Tonight was one of those nights.

"Anything suits me just fine, what did you have in mind?"

She heard the manure and wet bedding dropping into the barrow.

"I was thinking veggie burgers and homemade chocolate chip cookies and ice cream for dessert."

"That," said Noah, "sounds terrific." He paused to incline his head and smile handsomely at her. Her cheeks reddened. He rarely got picky and liked anything she offered to make. Regularly, it was to take the extra work off her mother's hands. It was a good thing she was productive in the kitchen.

By the time her arms threatened to disassemble themselves, all ten stalls were mucked, clean and ready -including a well swept barn aisle way, spotless.

The horses had been put outside -where three quarters of their day was spent- snatching at patches of grass.

Evening seemed to take its time and Noah started his dusty Ford pickup, brought it around and waited for Callie to jump in. With pressure on the gas pedal, they headed into town.

CHAPTER 2

Returning from picking up supplies, Noah and Callie had realized just how sneaky time could be.

They would be running a little late, but Callie was convinced she could brew up dinner in record time. Her mom would be home soon, and surely her father was already there. They had only stopped at a tack and diner for a quick drink, but the sky was already dimming as the sun set.

A forest of cottonwood trees bordered the road. Callie's idling mind ran away as she stared out the window. She never got worn-out of ogling at the wondrous scenic landscape of her beautiful Wyoming.

Open country, characterizing grasslands, bluffs and draws, meandering water courses that created additional wildlife, diverse terrain, alpine meadows, glacial carved valleys and rugged alpine peaks. Moreover, in the distance, was Bighorn Mountains with its sister range

of the Rocky Mountains with two peaks rising over 13,
000 feet and over a dozen in excess of 12,000 feet. Cloud
Peak Glacier could be seen actively at the top. It was her
outdoor paradise; she couldn't think of being anywhere
else. *I belong here.*

It was easy to picture herself with her lovable Romana,
running full speed and leaving every single fear, worry
and care behind her.

Not that I can complain, she thought.

Callie had her perfect home, two loving and caring
parents, a potential growing relationship with Noah Riley
and a good chance at becoming a world class natural horse
trainer. What she really wanted was to inherit and run
Silver Creek Ranch and make positive it continued on a
bright path to the future.

She was assertive that once she graduated and summer
arrived, she'd have all the time in the world to focus on
what she loved the most: horses. Callie vowed to be with
them now and forever.

Noah snapped her out of her vicarious reverie.

"Why is it that you never seem to have a more..." he
searched for the word, "constructive day at school?"

Callie swiveled in her seat to face him and shrugged. "I
don't have very many friends," she admitted. "But Angela's
my best friend and I'm more than all right with that. My
classes just don't intrigue me, I guess," she continued
explaining.

Speaking on the topic of school, she suddenly felt
the tugging urge to tell him about Andrew Dale, just

to see what he thought and observe his reaction. When she finished spilling about him, Noah's face puckered in displeasure and shook his head in disapproval. "That Dale character ought to learn a lesson on how to treat a lady," he said, frowning. "By the sounds of it, I'd say your best bet is to steer clear of him." His voice indicated more than just advice. It exposed a hint of protective warning. Unless she had interpreted it wrong.

Callie wasn't conclusive of what else to say, but she itched to ask how Noah and his father, Dakota Riley were holding up. She was concerned for him because things were difficult at home.

Ten years ago, Noah's mother, Laura Riley, had passed away to a better place after suffering and battling cancer. It struck the Rileys hard and since that day, Noah's father had picked up a drinking problem. It had been his 'solution' in numbing away the emotional pain and lashing reminders that hurled in his head. So many questions may have been burying him that he may have thought that the answers would be found at the bottom of every bottle.

In comparison, Noah's method of coping was much healthier. He would drive down to Silver Creek when the stress at home piled on and was too much and take Black Bear out on a ride; abandoning the hurt and the nagging burdens. Callie severely sympathized for him and knew how much effort he had given into opening up and telling her. She promised him that he could confide in her.

Noah sensed the apprehensive silence which was only

filled a little by the purring Ford. His forehead crumpled and he threw her a quizzical look.

She glared past the windshield, training her attention on an oncoming set of headlights from another vehicle. Oddly, it drifted to the side as if it were trying to swerve and miss something. But Callie couldn't be one hundred percent certain because it was at a hazy void still.

Strangely, it was almost as if she could feel the mystifying pressure of his boring eyes on her. But the last thing she wanted was to pry into his personal and confidential life.

"Is there something you want to say, Callie?" he asked gently.

Callie squirmed uncomfortably. How was she supposed to ask him? *Well, Noah, I was just curious on how you're holding up and if your father's getting any better.*

He would know she meant to imply his father's drinking problem, but she despised the impact it was having on him.

Rather than his eyes being attentive to the road, the ranch hand was studying Callie carefully, and virtually forgot he was driving.

She very slowly met his strained expression, wanting, earnestly, to blurt out the truth. She deeply cherished his whole being. Nevertheless, perhaps it just wasn't the time.

Before reality caught up with her, from the corner of Callie's eye she captured in startling view the suddenly fast impending vehicle she had spotted and used as a distraction. Only now could she decipher it more clearly.

A large battered Chevy with a one-horse trailer hooked to the back came blazing dangerously at them. The driver was unmistakably on the wrong side of the road.

Callie was glued to her seat in horror, amazed at how fleetingly fast it had reached them, utterly unexpected.

When she remembered to speak, she shrieked "Noah, look out!", but it was too late.

By the time Noah whipped his focus ahead -slamming the brakes in a bone shattering grip- the only thing Callie experienced next was the impact of collision, the shattering of window glass shards, the tipping of the ford and the horse trailer-scraping adjacent to the road. Following a deafening neigh and the warm rush of blood in her veins before her head hit the dashboard and a world of frightening darkness swallowed her up.

CHAPTER 3

C allie was drowning in disorientation. It was like the world had stopped turning.

Was she drifting in and out of consciousness? She wasn't sure. Then again, it was hugely difficult for her to even distinguish the difference between dreaming and reality at the given time.

There was ringing in her ears in conjunction with the violent thrumming of her heart aginst her ribs. She felt out of balance. That's because she was. The car had tipped side ways off the road in the grass from within meters of the trees.

Her extremely fragile body felt someone painfully shuffle beside her. Which is when she also realized her seat belt pinned her into place. Her head felt awfully warm, wet and sticky. Whatever it was -and she had a pretty good idea what- she decided not to find out. To Callie, she had lost her thoughts and any sense of straight thinking; all equilibrium lost.

"Callie?" she heard someone say.

To begin with, she didn't know why she was here. Secondly, the only thing she did know without question was that she was downright frightened and scared.

"Callie, can you hear me?" asked Noah from beside her. His voice was broken, tense and hard as stone. It was just as much frightened and panicked as she felt.

What had happened here? That was all she wanted to know.

"Callie, talk to me," pleaded Noah.

Who was he? Callie didn't know who he was or why she was with him. She felt broken, out of place and off kilter.

A strong grunt of pain overwhelmed an attemptive move from Noah which quickly made him settle back to the most bearable position.

Both of them could hear sirens far away but it quickly drove their ears to a more distinct noise. Bashing and thrashing against metal doors. The struggles of a terrified horse trying to escape the hell hole he had abruptly found himself in.

Callie knew that sound, surprisingly. She could recognize it. It was the one thing she could clearly carve out of her memory. The sound of a horse which she was briefly relieved to discover she was capable of remembering. She would hold on to it firmly, she promised herself.

All she held on to was the sound of the petrified horse. It pieced a vital part of her existence. Everything else she couldn't explain.

She wanted to set the horse free, let it break away from his metallic cavern and unrestrictingly flee from this chaos.

"Callie, talk to me. Please say something!" begged Noah frantically again.

She felt the stranger's hand on hers. With half closed eyes, her mind wavered painful obscured flashes she could not describe. Dizziness began to dominate her sight and her timid body told her to let it slip under and try to protect her from the pain. Callie thought it would be better to listen and drooped her eyes fully shut, giving in.

"Callie, no!" shouted Noah fiercely.

Leave me alone, thought Callie.

"Callie, wake up! Stay with me!"

The sirens grew louder. Her eyes inclined half way up once more with protest. She had to admit, she liked the sound of the stranger's voice. It was handsome and unusually familiar but she didn't worry about why. Again, her brain ordered her eyes locked.

"Callie Marie Marshall, you stay with me. Do you hear me? Stay awake!" he demanded.

More fear than authority coated his commanding voice. But Callie chose to listen to her body and wholly gave way to the weight of unconsciousness,

The last thing she recanted before the blackness swept over was the screaming horse which she could have sworn broke free of his metal cage and galloped out of sight, deep into the trees.

CHAPTER 4

Under her eyelids where she remained insentient, Callie's mind was in an up roaring daze. Her head felt tight and it hurt from the contact it had with the Ford's dashboard.

Somehow the darkness felt lighter to Callie. Less heavy, like she wasn't submerged under her mind's protective barriers as deeply. Was she waking up? Probably; if she could feel her ribs ache up a storm and her head pounding like a hammer, surely she was about to wake up. She felt closer to the surface of consciousness.

Intuitively, she knew it was safe. But prior to fluttering her eyes open, Callie's ears picked up on a couple of worried voices. She couldn't make out what they were saying. It was still muffled. Her brain refused to engage itself on processing the words.

Morbidly, she wondered what had happened to the stranger who had been with her. She knew they had obviously been in a car accident. But what she didn't know was how she ended up there. More than that, she wasn't certain as to who she really was. Except that she could easily recall a strong memory of horses.

The second the thought hit, she instantly remembered crashing against the metal trailer and the galloping of hooves that had amazingly escaped his prison trap.

Her concentration wasn't fuzzy either about remembering a dark, blood bay mare. Flowing black mane and tail, satin coat with a shining gleam up on a hill, gentle tempered eyes, perfectly conformed head and body...

In a flash the name came naturally off her lips, rolling out in a feeble croak, "Romana?"

The two voices she had been deliberately ignoring halted midsentence and she felt two pairs of eyes on her, ensued by her name. Now it was if her ears had been relieved of some obstruction and her hearing returned to normal.

"Callie Bear?" said an alarmed male voice.

"Callie, honey?" a female voice just as stressed as the first.

Callie flickered her eyelids and found herself staring at a bright white ceiling diffusely illuminated by florescent lighting. It was as if she had a hundred bruises all over her body or as if she had rammed against a brick wall. It was close enough. Stiffness kept her rigid.

The two visitors gawked at her with concerned eyes combined with relief. In one blink they hovered on each side of the bed. The beautiful woman -luxuriant coffee hair, deep, placid stormy grey eyes, well rounded face and rosy cheeks- holding her hand, and the kind man -rich, medium brown hair, honey brown eyes with tinges of amber, well-developed angular face- who was using his fingers to delicately comb the top of her wavy tressed hair.

Who were they? she wondered. Should she know them?

A doctor ambled in to the hospital room and the benevolent man stepped aside to allow her to be examined.

"Hi there, Callie," he spoke very friendly and calm. She gave him a waiting stare.

He had flaxen gold hair, contrasted nut-brown eyes and a refined dimensional face that displayed a sympathetic, understanding character which made him look like the perfect kind of doctor anyone could disclose with.

"My name is Dr. Kayden. Do you remember what happened?"

A wave of thoughtful reserve was cast over Callie as she tried to gather what had happened to her. Patiently, all three of them stood, looking expectantly.

The room felt weirdly crowded all of a sudden. What she felt like saying was that she had a huge hole in her brain and like she was missing such a massive part of her life. But instead she sadly shook her head. "No," she mumbled. "I don't remember anything." Her mind dithered around for her memory without success.

Dejection brushed over the couple while the doctor observed something in quiet. Then, he turned to face the couple who now consoled each other at the end of her bed. Callie wished she knew who they were. Possibly related?

"Mr. and Mrs. Marshall, may I speak with you outside for just a moment?"

They glanced in unison at Callie and then back to Dr. Kayden, nodding.

"Callie," said Dr. Kayden, "We'll be right back."

She didn't reply but nodded, too. The three of them shuffled out the door and closed it behind them.

Callie sat still and quiet, desperate for some sort of explanation. Answers. The doctor's voice hushingly carried through the slit at the bottom of the door, but she didn't want to pay attention. What she sought was to see Romana and escape the confinement of this compelling atmosphere.

Adjusting herself upright, she winced a little and truly surveyed herself physically. Exactly how much had she been damaged, not only physically, but emotionally and mentally?

There was a gauze bandage on her forehead which felt tender underneath. Her ribs were wrapped securely all around, so she suspected broken ribs. The rest of her remained at a very sore state with distributed bruises and mere cuts already on the mend.

Poor Callie pushed to pick through her head and remember but it was no use. It was like trying to find her way out of a maze blindfolded, which did little to comfort her.

The silver doorknob revolved and in came Dr. Kayden

and the Marshalls as she remembered was their last names. They had called her Callie. So clearly that was her name. Imaginings of her mare, Romana, popped up and then she instantaneously thought of the fetching stranger at the scene of the accident again. When she passed his memory, it made her restless.

"Callie, sweetie," said Mrs. Marshall with dry tears smeared on her face. She swept aside strands of her hair and tucked it behind her ear, warily probing her daughter. "We know you don't remember much or maybe even anything..." -Callie could tell the sad woman was struggling- "But we need to know if you recognize us. Do you remember at all who we are?" she almost pleaded. Her husband held her hand and squeezed it.

Callie contained a hunch of who they were.

"I think so," she tried, pulling her eyebrows together in hard concentration. "You're my...parents, right? Cause then I must be Callie Marshall, your daughter?" She wished it was legitimate certainty instead of it coming out like guessing questions. But it seemed enough to loosen their troublesome expressions.

"Anything else you remember?" encouraged her father hopefully.

"Do I have a horse named Romana? It's the one thing I am sure about," she frowned.

Her parents nodded, their spirits elevating just an increment.

"And the escaping horse from the trailer?"

They all displayed nonplussed confusion.

"What escaping horse?" asked Lilly.

"Um, never mind..." she said. It *must have just been my imagination*, she thought privately. Could it have been? If the entire accident was blocked from her memory, how come she could retract that part so easily? The workings of her mind were complicated.

"Callie," interrupted Dr. Kayden, "I understand this is very overwhelming, but we looked at your tests and we believe you have post-traumatic amnesia. Now you might have what's known as "islands of memory", which explains why you can recall only certain things and not others. We also believe that moments before the car accident and at the time of the accident can't be retrieved from your memory because of a brief interruption of your short and long-term memory transfer mechanism. The good news is you have a very good chance of recovering it, but the bad news is we aren't entirely sure when that is. We're positive it was a result of the head injury you acquired on impact. It's going to take time.

"Your parents will be able to take you home as soon as we run some more tests. You'll need a lot of bed rest and make sure to take it easy within the next few weeks. You gained a head concussion so any time you feel dizzy, nauseated, or experience bad headaches, impaired balance, speech problems, things like that, I'd like you to report to me immediately."

"Of course," said her father.

A moment slipped by when Callie noticed someone standing out in the hall, staring at her in the door frame.

He seemed familiar but yet she didn't know who he was. She admitted to herself that he was very handsomely attractive but his entire complexion was pale and extremely bothered. He had cuts and bruises on his face and arms, and wore a black t-shirt with dark blue jeans. His eyes were so fused on hers that she peeled away from his scrutiny and pretended to look elsewhere.

When tests were finished, Callie got dressed into clothes her parents had brought in: a short-sleeved, brown flannel shirt, tight blue denim jeans and a pair of Abilene cowgirl boots.

Callie felt the fresh cool air skim the surface of her exposed skin as she walked out of Wyoming Medical Center and mounted the back of the pickup's window seat.

David got behind the wheel and Lilly settled into shotgun. Before wheeling home, her dad gazed past the windshield as if he were waiting on someone.

And he was.

The handsome cowboy glided out the doors and right into the truck, opposite end of Callie, avoiding eye contact. Callie froze and no one dared breathed a word. The truck was put into motion.

Rolling home, Callie suddenly felt afraid and stiffened at the realization of who sat beside her.

CHAPTER 5

C allie stared into the empty darkness as she lay undeniably restless on her bed.

Above her headboard hanging on the wall was her favorite item in the room: a large, stunning dream catcher with a gorgeous dun blanket appaloosa stallion running majestically in the sunset. She adored her room's center piece.

Her parents were fast asleep and the only thing that kept her from sneaking out the front door and into the barn was that she might get caught. Primarily because she assumed it was against the rules to be out of the house this late at night; especially considering doctor's orders for bed rest.

"Bed rest my hiney," muttered Callie. It felt more like quarantine.

Throughout the rest of the day she had worked on gathering information about herself. She was seventeen, her full name was Callie Marie Marshall, she lived on Silver Creek Ranch in Natrona County, Wyoming, and her parents were Lilly and David Marshall. Her birthday was on September 18. She had also learned about her ownership of Bailey and Panther, who both slept at ease. Bailey at her feet and Panther on the carpet sprawled across the wooden floor.

Best of all, considered Callie, she had a beautiful horse who she was dying to visit. The longer she stalled, the more agitated she got and that unsettled her. The Labradors, sensing her edginess, woke up and gazed at her. Panther skidded to her bedroom door as if to read her mind.

She smirked. "Well," she told the boys, "I could always say you two needed to go to the bathroom." It was a weak scheme but Callie dismissed it and propped herself carefully out of bed.

All day long, she had fought to stay positive and optimistic. It hadn't soared as high as she'd been planning.

The drive home from the hospital had been completely awkward and overwrought with tension. Her parents had avoided speaking to her the whole way back, worried that they'd be putting too much pressure on her by saying anything. It was best to leave her be. To leave her think.

Noah on the other hand had caused the most tension. He hadn't released his eyes on her until the truck had pulled up into the ranch and she was very distraught about it; if that hadn't been bad enough, she had flinched when she saw a horse trailer pass by them which had caused her to feel nervous.

"I really have no choice," she whispered to the dogs as she slipped on her denims from the hospital and kept on her Mustang t-shirt. "I'm just going to have to deal with this. Whatever happened to me, I'm going to fix it." Her evident assertiveness transferred to the dogs and they pawed at the door impatiently.

"Shhh," hissed Callie quietly. "You'll wake mom and dad up."

Lacing up her pasture boots she twisted the door knob and tiptoed down the stairs, sneaking an apple from the kitchen table's fruit basket on the way out and literally slithered through the narrow gap successfully. Tailing behind, Bailey and Panther nipped mischievously heading down to the barn.

The night was cool and still. No humidity was present to spoil it. Moonlight assisted Callie to find her way more simply and she switched the barn lights on.

An eruption of contentment washed over her and felt right at home, even if most of her memory was like looking through a fogged up window.

Ten stirring horses peered finely shaped heads over their stall doors and supplied Callie with curious looks as if to say: *Do you know what time it is?*

The canine troublemakers disappeared into the tack room.

Spotting Romana, who was located at the far left end of the aisle way, Callie didn't take her time to the mare's stall despite her grouchy injuries. Romana nickered excitedly, adding a bob of her divinely defined head for good measure.

Her horse whuffled Callie's hand with a soft velvety muzzle and lipped the juicy, ripe apple right off. A midnight treat was an unexpected delight but acceptable nonetheless. If Callie hadn't known any better, the dark, blood bay tossed her head proudly at her stable buddies just to gloat.

Rubbing and stroking her satiny neck felt comforting and wonderfully relaxing. Just the feel of it was like emotional therapy.

Sleep seemed pointless and unachievable to Callie since she had been resting endlessly it seemed. To go about recovering her memory, she far from knew. However, she would hope that with time the puzzle would piece together and show her the full picture she was failing to see.

"I've really missed you, Romana."

Her mare's eyes forthcomingly gazed at her and her ears pricked forward to keep aware of her leader's words.

Talking to Romana when no one else would listen, or when she perfectly knew she would keep all of her secrets was the greatest feeling. Her horse was always there for her.

Callie sighed. "It's so much easier to talk to you about anything. People are much more complicated."

Romana snorted softly.

"You're more affordable than a therapist," she chuckled.

Then, she changed the subject. "I need to find that horse. He's out there somewhere, and I'm going to find him." Callie hoped that he was safe wherever he was.

She hugged her horse and sighed heavily again. "You

make me feel so much better. Thanks for being there for me."
She closed her eyes and focused on embracing her horse.

When she parted, Callie checked her watch. "Maybe I should go back up to bed," she told Romana, a little paranoid. She half-expected her mom or dad to pop into view. Or maybe both.

Disagreeing, Romana nudged at her and then backed away from the stall door. Callie unlatched the bolt and slipped inside, embracing her special creature in another loving hug and always pleased when she wanted her to stay.

It wasn't the greatest idea, cause she was bound to get in trouble, but Callie sat in the straw and leaned her back and head against the wall facing the mare, who then came to lower her neck and rest her muzzle on top of Callie's shoulder. She inhaled deeply and exhaled with a huff.

"I'll close my eyes for just a few minutes. I shouldn't stay much longer, girl."

She did just that, except by the time she reopened her eyes, morning sunlight was streaming through the stall windows. She sleepily staggered to her feet, alarmed, and checked the time. Seven O'clock in the morning.

Callie had dreamed of the feral horse last night. Dreamed he was a beautiful mustang just like the one on her dream catcher. Wildly galloping in the grasslands and past the Bighorn mountains. She dreamed of him stopping to drink from Indian Creek -one of the water courses near her home-just as the sun was setting, where he then trotted freely away and into the night. Then, she had a second dream of a historical herd of horses that were bred by a master tribe of Native Americans. One of the first to truly develop an astonishing American breed: the Appaloosa. An entire herd of Appaloosa horses ran in her dream and their hooves pounded on the earth like drums, until finally she had woken up.

She spun on her heels and clomped into the aisle way. Romana stared after her.

"I'll be right back, girl. Don't worry," Callie promised.

The mare's ears twitched and swiveled in the direction of the barn entrance. Then, Callie heard footsteps and whirled to see which of her parents had awakened. It was neither.

In her direction came strolling Noah Riley.

CHAPTER 6

Butterflies and tethered knots assaulted Callie's
stomach. Her back stiffened as the handsome
cowboy stranger strode toward her wearing jeans and a
dark grey t-shirt which marginally snugged around his
torso and arms, making visible his well rounded, but
wiry biceps and firm stomach. On his head he wore a
black Stetson and appeared more fresh and organized in
comparison to the last time she saw him, which was at the
hospital. He even had more color in his cheeks now and
his minor cuts, like hers, were also on the mend.

Callie tried to put her finger on something that was
bothering her. Why had he been there?

Her eyes popped wide. He was the stranger who
had been in the car with her! It seemed she had to keep
reminding herself of this and stop being so surprised. Did
he work here? Was he friendly and nice? Her heart raced
as he paced closer.

The cowboy's footfalls halted in front of her. Nervously she inclined her eyes and met his. He was wearing a pained expression which, for a peculiar reason, hurt her to see him like that. That manifested feature didn't belong there.

"Er... Hi, Callie. I'm Noah Riley. You, uh, probably don't remember me but I work here. I heard about your amnesia..." -he said the last word with a forced effort like he was unwillingly admitting to something he didn't want to deal with- "And I'm really, really sorry."

"I remember you," Callie murmured.

Noah's face slightly lifted at that.

"You were in the car with me right? But... that's all I remember," she said apologetically.

His face fell as if he had expected her to say something different and she had disappointed him.

It wasn't intentional, but Callie didn't know what to say.

"How are you feeling?" he asked after a while of awkward silence.

"Sore," replied Callie.

He laughed without humor, almost dryly, but she could see that he was trying. "Yeah, I know how you feel there."

"But I'm glad to be alive."

Noah nodded in agreement.

"So, you work here? What do you do?"

"I'm a ranch hand. I work for your father to take care of the ranch and all the horses and cattle." He paused.

"You really don't remember much, do you?" he mumbled, downcast. His eyes looked like they were crumbling inside, revealing the feelings going on inside of him.

Callie shook her head. "I wish I did, but it's just too hard."

Noah sent her a gentle, sympathetic look.

She liked this boy.

"You certainly remember Romana well."

"I'm not sure why that is," shrugged Callie. "But I can't say I'm not happy about it."

A half-hearted smile crossed Noah's lips.

As if suspecting they were speaking of her, the Thoroughbred Quarter Horse mare creeped her neck over the stall door and stomped her foot demanding Callie's attention.

Callie carefully carried her achy body to Romana and caught her muzzle between her hands and gave it a genuine kiss.

The ranch hand's smile spread out a little more.

"Morning!"

Their heads both snapped up at the greeting. Callie jumped a little. Striding in came Adrian.

Coming to stand next to Noah, he eyed her uncomprehensively. "Hey there, Callie."

She couldn't explain reasoning, but she knew exactly who he was. Adrian Farren, the other ranch hand of Silver Creek Ranch, and also her father's best friend and a good friend of the family.

"How ya holdin' up, Kiddo?"

"I'm doing the best I can," she mouthed truthfully. "How's Darla?" she asked, shocking Adrian senseless at the question. Noah was stunned and speechless.

"She's great, Callie. You remember Darla?"

Darla Hue Farren -undulating, golden brown hair cropped to her shoulders and side sweep bangs, cinnamon brown eyes and a glittering white smile that brightened the entire world- was Adrian's wife and always had accompanied Lilly and Callie on trips to town for lunch or occasionally stopped by Silver Creek to join them for dinner. Darla loved French braiding Callie's hair and even attended her on trail rides on her days off from her job as owner down at Hue Farren's Tack & Diner.

Callie adored their homemade style ice cream which she didn't forget was her favorite dessert. In fact, Darla had taught her how to make it in returning favor of having Callie run her through her famous chocolate chip cookie recipe.

Additionally, Callie also remembered that Darla was like a second mom to her. Or at least it felt that way. Anything she ever needed, Darla accepted in helping her with eager open arms. She had such a strong, sparkling personality and, like Angela, had a positive, optimistic outlook on life. She had told Callie once, "It's like Yogi Berra use to say, 'If you don't know where you are going, you might wind up someplace else'". It was one of the many things Callie valued about Darla. Not only was she full of life, but she fulfilled life with her qualities.

One time Darla had gone riding out in the summer

on Bandit with Callie and Romana and had given her words of wisdom when she was down -which she still held on to till this day. "Never let anyone tell you 'you can't', because you *can*. Hold your head up, Callie, and always know that absolutely no one has the right to stop you from going after your dreams. And if they try, well..." she winked, "just give them a good kick in the keg!"

"Yes, I remember Darla." Callie searched for some uncomplicated explanation, but without luck.

Adrian was perplexed. But Noah was hit hard by the fact that she didn't remember who he was at all -and not just as the stranger in the car with Callie at the time of the accident.

"Well, I'll be," breathed Adrian. "Suppose it's selective, that memory loss of yours?" He didn't wait for her to answer. "We're sure glad you're all right, Callie. We were all worried for ya."

Noah dropped his eyes from Callie.

"Excuse me," he said. "I'd better get to work," and vanished into the feed room.

"Good idea," said Adrian. "See you soon, Callie." With a tip of the brim of his Stetson, Adrian dispatched.

Out of the blue, Callie had suddenly felt like she had hurt Noah Riley's feelings.

With one final pat on Romana's crest, she dragged herself up to the house with a bucket full of guilt.

CHAPTER 7

A week had passed when Callie finally felt confident
enough to return to school.

She knew, though, that it'd be like arriving at a new
school all over again. And there was only three weeks left
of it.

She couldn't shake the nagging idea of what Adrian
had said in the barn a week ago.

Suppose it's selective, that memory loss of yours?

His voice echoed for a thousandth repetitious time.

After breakfast, Callie got dressed for school; pulling
on a top, a pair of jeans and Kayland Convert hiking
boots, grabbing her backpack on the way out.

Her ribs had been healing well, and there had been
only a few sleepless nights she had had to tolerate. She
only had to put up with one bad migraine that sent her
to bed early. When she had managed to fall asleep that
particular night, she dreamed of a trailer with a frightened

horse inside who escaped into the trees with desperate screams. Callie dreamt of him wandering helpless and alone through the woods, hurt or maybe worse.

She trotted out the door and to her bus stop. The whole way down, Romana had followed her half-way till she situated herself atop a large hill and watched her leader sidle from the fence and out of sight. She'd wait to carry Callie the rest of the way home.

Mom had made her lunch and Dad had called the school to inform them of her return. Callie was nervous and felt as skittish as a horse for school but forced positive thoughts out so she could spare herself a stressful day.

Angela had phoned her on Saturday night and Callie had remembered her best friend fairly well. She was relieved that she wouldn't need to feel all alone. She couldn't repress a smile as soon as Angela caught view of her and patted the empty space next to her. Angie didn't even wait to say hi.

"Callie! I've missed you, girl!"

"Hi, Angie," said Callie, not able to quaver the feeling that various set of eyes were on her. She refused to take a chance and find out. Who cared if they stared? She hadn't done anything wrong.

The bus geared in motion.

"You can't believe how freaked out I was after I heard about the accident. And the amnesia? I thought you'd forget your best friend!" she ranted. "How do you feel?"

"Better," said Callie. Half of it was true. "I only remember some things and not others."

Angela hesitated. "You don't remember the accident at all?"

"No," said Callie shaking her head. She did remember the mysterious horse running away into the forest, but anything else she couldn't grasp.

"Andrew's been asking about you," said Angela changing the subject. "Do you remember him?"

Callie tried to, but shook her head again. The name didn't ring a bell.

"Well, don't worry," Angela dismissed. "All you need to know is to stay away from Andrew Dale. He's a big mean jerk and you don't like him."

Callie frowned. "I don't?"

"Nope, whatsoever. And with good reason."

"Hmm." Then something dawned on Callie and she groaned. "I'll have to catch up on so much homework!"

"No problem! What are best friends for? I'll catch you up like that!" Angela snapped her fingers under Callie's nose.

Great, thought Callie, *Can't wait.*

First class had been steady, but not short enough. On her way back down to second period, Callie mused over all the school work. Worst part was, she didn't remember a thing which resulted in her feeling utterly lost. She could only imagine what the rest of her classes would be like.

Angela was in two of her classes, Biology and English, but she offered to help anyway.

By now, news had spread about Callie's accident and circulated the entire building. Most students didn't even know Callie personally. However, they knew enough to recognize her.

When she left second, she hardly even noticed Andrew trailing behind to her locker until she opened it and he pulled up at her side.

"Hey, Callie." He said.

Callie surveyed this tall stranger. Angela had failed to mention what he looked like, exactly. But she was about to find out.

"Um, hi. Do I know you?" she asked, sliding school books into her locker to lighten her load.

"It's Andrew. Andrew Dale." He smiled innocently.

So this was who Angela talked about. Callie kept cautious, reminding herself that her friend had said she wasn't suppose to like him.

"How are you doing?" he said, attempting small talk.

"Good," replied Callie.

"That's great. Well, I was just wondering," said Andrew -pausing and wavering the question- "if maybe you might want to be my... date for prom next week?" His voice sounded so hopeful that Callie actually felt guilty.

He didn't seem too bad. Maybe it wouldn't hurt. What harm would it do?

"Sure, Andrew," she accepted the request. "I'll go to prom with you."

Somehow she felt Angela wouldn't approve but neither could she locate the problem.

Andrew flashed a grin so wide; Callie literally thought he might permanently set it on his face.

"Great!"

The bell rang for next period.

"See you later, Callie!" He practically bounced to his next class with happiness.

She waved, "Bye," and plowed her way to class, too.

Eighty minutes later, Callie marched out the doors to have lunch and enjoy the good sunny weather.

Her classmates couldn't all help but prattle about upcoming graduation three weeks from now. Graduation could wait. One thing she was dying to do was hop on Romana and go for a long wanted ride. It seemed like most of her hours were spent brooding over Noah and asking herself what she had done wrong.

A ride could allow her a temporary break.

Though, if Noah wasn't mad at her, he sure didn't act like it. What exactly had she done to upset him? Whatever it was, she hadn't meant to. Maybe it would be best to confront him. All week, unless it was necessary to talk to her, Noah had avoided conversation and Callie was weighed down with guilt and confusion.

The accident could have been avoided, she thought. Or maybe that's what she wanted to convince herself. Maybe Noah did, too. Noah had been behind the wheel from what she recalled. Could he be blaming himself for what happened?

Then, there was a tugging nuisance at Callie's heart about the horse. She just couldn't let it go. What had happened to him? Was he lost or hurt? In a way she wanted to find him, but that seemed next to impossible; considering it had been a while since the accident and he could be anywhere by now. That didn't stop her from wanting it badly.

She sat on a bench and unwrapped her sandwich, taking one bite before Angela came into existence and perched herself next to Callie. Her friend gave her a befuddled expression.

"What?"

"You're going to prom with Andrew?" she said incredulously. Even for naturally positive and optimistic Angela Raymond, Callie wasn't accustomed to her disapproving tone.

"Yes..." said Callie.

Angie raised an eyebrow.

Callie put her sandwich down. "I felt sorry for him. He doesn't seem so bad. Really," she said defensively.

"Callie Marshall," said Angela, sounding like a disappointed parent utilizing their child's first and last name when they were in trouble. "How hard did you hit your head? Andrew can't be trusted. He's taking advantage of you."

"It's just for one night," Callie pointed out. "It's not like I'm marrying the guy."

"Tell that to him," Angie sniffed.

Callie frowned, then sighed. "I can't just cancel on him. One night won't kill me. Besides, once we graduate, I'm likely never to see him again."

"Okay," said Angela, doubtful. "But I sure hope you know what you're getting yourself into."

⇥⇥⇥

Like expected, Romana had been waiting for Callie up at the hill to carry her home.

Until doctor's orders, Callie wasn't suppose to be riding at all, but she shook it off and decided that if her mare only walked it was harmless. Both her parents had gone to town to shop for groceries, anyhow.

Bailey and Panther tagged right along.

Taking a nice shower was a great remedy for her muscles and her still-healing ribs. The hot water splashed her skin and trickled down the drain. But it was a mere excuse to avoid going into the barn in case Noah happened to be there, which of course he was.

She couldn't just dodge him on a constant basis. Sooner or later they both had to face what had happened to them and move on. And Callie was working on regaining her memory in any way she could.

She shut off the water and jumped out, sealed herself in a towel and darted to her room.

She glanced out the window only to flush tomato red in the cheeks when she caught Noah readjusting a fence and stopped to peer up at her.

Swiftly, Callie backed away from the window, embarrassed, and retrieved some clothes. With her pair of jeans, she wore a cotton, hand-dyed horse t-shirt with a printed scene of horses in a cavern called "Passage"

-she knew she had an obsession, but Darla ordered them specially for her online all the time- laced her pasture boots and fastened her half-chaps on top.

"What can I say?" she told Bailey and Panther as they waited for her. "If I'm going to be obsessed about horses, I might as well go all out, don't ya think?"

The dogs barked in concord as Callie grabbed her brown Stetson cowgirl hat -for a change- on the way out this time.

There wasn't much that she could do until she completely recovered physically. Mom and Dad refused to let her lift heavy objects and told her that she could do the simple chores. Feed and groom the horses, sweep the barn, tidy the tack room, etc.

Since she felt the urge to stall for a little while longer before speaking to Noah, Callie sauntered over to the pasture which the horses were kept. She balanced over one of the boards on her feet and leaned over.

In the herd, who Callie loved so dearly, her dark, blood bay mare's outline was easily identifiable.

Sensing Callie's automatic presence, Romana excitedly stalked toward the fence. Her coat beamed in brilliance streaked with sunlight and her coarse jet black mane flowed in a fluid motion above her crest.

Right behind her followed Black Bear, Star the bay, Denver the liver chestnut, the lovely paint Bandit, Silver Creek's buckskin Trigger, Bliss the albino mare with pretty blue eyes, Daisy the Palomino, Lady the Appaloosa, and Mocha with all the glory a brown gruella has to offer.

Callie laughed. "I'd say we have enough for a party," she joked.

Silver Creek Ranch and all its horses meant the world to Callie.

She saw Noah vanish into the barn.

She divided her attention and affection between all of them. But Romana was determined to steal it all for herself.

Callie chuckled. "Silly mare."

Happy with a few pats and scratches, each horse, excluding Romana, retrieved back to their patches of grass.

"I'll be riding you soon, girl," promised Callie.

Like her words processed into horse language, her horse whinnied in the direction of Silver Creek's wonderful trails, with Bighorn Mountains hiding behind the trees.

"Soon," she reminded the mare with one last rub.

With one big breath, she twirled around and headed for the barn.

CHAPTER 8

C allie scooted into the barn, squaring her shoulders and trying to insolate her nervous jitters.

She found him in the tack room cleaning Black Bear's striking western saddle with top quality leather and hand craftsmanship and appealing silver plating; his rhythmic scrubbing seamed trance-like to her.

Noah's black Stetson shaded his eyes and was unaware of her standing there. Only when he went to grab more saddle soap did he realize he had company.

"Oh," he said surprised. "Hey Callie." He didn't walk back to his saddle.

His attention became transfixed. Callie scanned his hazel eyes, trying to read his thoughts.

"Hey." She hesitated in the doorway, and then took a step. "Need any help?" Might as well approach the subject slowly, she thought.

"Sure. You're welcome to do Bear's bridle." His face

was marked with a sort of reserved caution, wary to expose any of his emotions.

Callie stripped the black leather brow band bridle from its hold and hung it over in the center hook and began working from the headstall to the bit, curb strap and finally the reins. Both had been so absorbed in their tasks that she finally overdrew the silence by sucking in a deep breath.

"Noah," said Callie, "we need to talk."

He stiffened, but she went on. She kept her eyes to the ground while he fused his into hers. This was harder than she thought.

"What's the matter, Cowgirl? You look like you've committed a crime," he teased lightly. The strain in his voice couldn't be hidden.

She mustered herself and lifted her timid eyes. "I'm really sorry if I hurt your feelings and I don't blame you for being angry with me," she blurted, each word tripping over the other.

Noah raised his eyebrows. "Angry with you? Callie," he shook his head dubiously, "why would I be angry with you? You didn't do anything wrong."

Callie wrinkled her forehead. "You're... not?"

Noah pursued a few tiny steps of reassurance. "Why did you assume I was mad at you?"

"I'm not sure. It's just, you really haven't talked to me all week and I thought maybe it had something to do with that day you found me in the barn with Romana."

He thought for a moment before he answered and returned to his saddle, polishing it absently.

"I was upset because you remember Adrian and Darla. Then you regained your memory of David and Lilly. You even remember Angela and Romana. You remember the horse from the trailer at the accident somehow. But..." he gripped the cloth in his hand firmly as his emotions rose to the surface, the tendons in his arms standing out.

"But what?" whispered Callie.

He sighed as if in defeat, gazing up at her gently. "But you can't remember me," he said at last.

That stung her, even if it hadn't been meant to.

"I don't understand it. I've regained quite a deal of memory, but there's still a lot I don't remember. Mostly the accident. It's like when you talk about it, it's hard to believe it ever really happened." To evade eye contact, Callie worked away on Bear's bridle.

"It's not your fault, Callie. I just overreacted. Besides," Noah glanced up again, "you'll get your full memory back. Just wait and see. I'm sorry I made you worry all week." His face brightened up and Callie relaxed a little.

"I don't know," she smiled playfully. "You might need to owe me for the sleep deprivation."

"And how do you reckon I should do that?" laughed Noah.

She weighed her options internally before responding with a widespread grin. Noah eyed her suspiciously.

"You, Noah Riley, are going to take me on a trail ride."

"Callie," Noah protested, "I really don't think this is a good idea. You heard what the doctor said and your parents would flip a lid."

He reluctantly swung his freshly clean saddle over Black Bear's velvet back and unwillingly cinched it up snuggly around the gelding's belly.

Callie wasn't biting. "Nonsense, besides, it's almost neglect having to keep my poor mare trapped in the pasture all day long," she argued. "And I feel fine. Wouldn't it be considered responsible since I asked you to come along? Not to babysit of course, but strictly a favor to the horses?"

Romana happily anticipated a ride and pranced on the spot excitedly while Callie comfortably snugged up the girth and adjusted her stirrups.

Noah shook his head doubtfully. "Your folks are gonna blow a gasket."

"Yes, they can flip a lid, blow a gasket, cry 'wolf' or even make steam come out of their ears. I'll take full responsibility. But I've been dying for a good ride. So please don't spoil this for me. I'll deal with the heat later."

Surely enough, Noah gave in and took the bait. "Okay, but not for too long. The last thing I need is to loose my job."

They led the horses out and swung themselves over their backs.

Callie could feel her mare bunched with energy just crying to be let loose. A good gallop was the perfect medicine for her. She didn't need, or want, anything else.

Noah settled and they trotted off down the path, trekking for the adventurous wilderness of Wyoming.

Callie caught Adrian watching them. Instead of interjecting, he shook his head chuckling, winked at them and waved till they disappeared.

CHAPTER 9

Romana snorted with pleasure as they rode through the endless copse of trees, soft dirt under her thudding hooves.

Bear perked his ears and replied with an agreeing nicker.

Callie peeped at Noah. "I'd say I was sorry," she smiled. "But I'm not."

"I figured as much," said Noah, entertained.

Soon, the dirt trail turned into a long stretch of grassy plains that Callie adored. They took their time up to Indian Creek. Callie had chosen this direction on purpose. Maybe her dream had been trying to tell her something. It was a long shot, but just maybe she'd see the mysterious horse.

It was endlessly beautiful here.

Romana impatiently broke into a canter and Bear didn't even wait for Noah to ask him before he speedily treaded behind her.

"Callie... We shouldn't be cantering. You'll end up getting hurt. You shouldn't even be riding in the first place."

"Lighten up, Cowboy," said Callie. His black Quarter horse snorted loudly as if to back her up.

"I can't believe I let you talk me into this," he muttered as he fluently rocked to the three-beat gait.

The horses were lost in their beauty, power and momentum. But they did not lack an ounce of grace. They stretched out their powerful legs to ground-eating strides.

Without warning, Callie watched the mare's ears flicker rapidly toward the forest and elevated her head to crane it in that direction when she suddenly saw a ghostly flash of movement within the cover of the shadows. She thoroughly scoured and brought Romana to an abrupt halt.

Bear also jostled to a standstill next to her. Noah looked puzzled.

"Why'd you stop?"

"There's something in the woods."

"How do you know?"

"I saw it move behind the trees over there behind the bushes," she gestured.

Noah took scout into the trees now, too. "Are you sure?"

"I have two eyes, don't I?" she breathed, aggrivated.

Callie asked Romana to walk on and steered her to where she had seen the spectral action from the unknown lurker.

Is it you, pretty horse? Callie far from knew what the horse actually looked like, but any horse to her eyes was beautiful.

Noah stayed where he was, even though Bear wanted to follow.

A few meters down she looked to the left and right; nothing but cottonwood trees and Indian paintbrush wildflowers that were inconspicuously enveloped by bright flowerlike bracts. Her heart fell with deterrence and she tried to dislodge it. She was going to find him, no matter what it took. She knew he was out there and she wouldn't give up because her conscience persisted on the idea that he needed her. She wouldn't renounce that desire, either.

Dismally, she toddled Romana to stand next to Noah again.

"C'mon," said Noah, glancing at his watch. "We need to get back. Your parents will be home soon."

Callie sighed but knew he was right. They spun the horses around.

Callie suddenly smirked. "I'll race ya back, Cowboy!"

"You're on!"

They bolted fast for home and laughed, the horses charging neck and neck.

"Romana and I are going to kick your butt!" hollered Callie.

Noah immediately stopped laughing and leaned more into the saddle.

"Not a chance Callie Marshall!"

"I told you," said Callie as her and Noah unvarnished the saddles and placed them on their stout racks. "Romana hates to be beat in a race. That's just the way it is." She almost looked smug, but tried to hide it.

"That mare has some speed, I'll admit."

"*Some* speed? Ha," she scoffed. "My mare could outrun a purebred Thoroughbred racehorse!"

Noah chuckled and held his arms up in surrender. "You're absolutely right," he agreed. "Now let's get to the house. I can almost smell the food now!"

Callie's mouth watered as soon as he spoke the word. Her parents had made it home first, so she'd have to explain to them about her and Noah's little outing on the trails. She could tell Noah seemed nervous about it.

By the time dinner was ready and the table had been set for the usual five people fix, everyone eagerly took their seats and said Grace.

Lilly always executed a perfect, heart-warming prayer of thanksgiving.

"Dear Lord," she said while everyone bowed their heads and closed their eyes. "Thank you for providing us with this wonderful food today, with each other and this brilliant ranch. We deeply say thanks for our marvelous horses and kindly thank you for the graciousness you have offered us."

And thank you for Romana and Noah, added Callie internally.

"Amen," they all ended.

Callie cautiously took small bites of her steak, potatoes and green beans. Yet, her parents mentioned nothing about the ride. Surely they would have elucidated for themselves, right?

She hated going behind their backs and breaking any of their rules, but it had been desperately needed. She wondered if Adrian had said something in regards about it.

But they all seemed to be chattering away about other things. Callie felt like the bomb would probably drop soon enough.

"Wow! Good eatin', Lilly!" complimented Adrian.

"Just wait till dessert," said Lilly with a pleased grin. As she scraped her chair back and collected everyone's empty plates, she eyed Callie before waning into the kitchen.

Callie silently groaned. That was all she needed to confirm it.

Then her mom came back with glare eating stares directed right at the giant dishes she carried filled with strawberry rhubarb and huckleberry pie.

"Holy crow, Mrs. Marshall!" exclaimed Noah. "Do those ever look tasty! I don't think I'll have a problem fitting those in here," he tapped his still-flat stomach.

Callie stifled a giggle, but Noah's eyeballs veered at her and his lips warped into a thrilled smile.

"I bet they don't just look tasty," threw in David Marshall.

Callie would shrug it off, enjoy dessert and face the music after when she helped her mother wash the dishes.

The rhubarb and pie were sliced into thick pieces to hand off around the table. She took her time to chew and swallow, savoring every bite. It was satisfyingly delicious, and she couldn't take another morsel if she tried.

Callie stacked all the empty dessert plates and trudged into the kitchen to help her mom. She started the hot water and soap while Lilly filled the other sink with clean rinsing water.

"So, how was your day?" asked Lilly casually.

Callie kept her eyes on the soapy dishes in the sink. "It was great. You know, school's the usual and all, but it was great," she repeated. "I agreed to go to prom with Andrew," she added hoping to sidetrack her mother a little longer.

"Andrew Dale?" her mom frowned. "I thought you didn't like that boy. Didn't you say something about him being very..." -she tried to wrack her brain for the word- "self-centered?"

Callie shrugged slightly. "I don't remember, and besides, he actually seems nice. It's only one night. What harm will it do? I already told Angela; it's not like I'm marrying the guy."

As she cleared and sponged the plates, cups, and utensils of their grime and stuck on left over food, she handed them to her mother and Lilly rinsed them to ready them for drying.

"Angela's heart is in the right place. I'm sure she's just trying to look out for you." She gave her daughter a thoughtful stare.

"I know she is," granted Callie. "But it's hard because I still don't remember most things and it's frustrating. I know I'll have a good time at prom," she tried self-assuredly. "I'll give Andrew a chance."

Lilly smiled indisputably. A fragment of silence sneaked on them before Callie couldn't take it any more and broke it.

"Mom, I know that I shouldn't have been riding," she started, "and I'm really sorry. I just couldn't be away from the saddle any longer. It was torturously killing me! But if it's any consolation," she blabbered, "Noah, of course, came with me and I feel completely fine. Physically, I mean."

"Yes, I know," Mom replied calmly. "Adrian informed me but told me not to worry. I had a gut feeling no one would be able to keep you off for much longer. And you can let Noah know that I appreciate him keeping you company," she smiled genuinely.

Translation: *You can let Noah know that I appreciate him for keeping a watchful eye on you.*

However, a very relieved Callie didn't press into a protest about it.

"Honey," continued her mother as she started drying. "I know it's been very difficult losing your memory. And I'm glad you've recovered some of it, but try to stay positive, okay? I know you'll remember everything with time and it will all turn out okay."

They enclosed in a hug.

"Thanks Mom."

CHAPTER 10

F riday morning at school, Callie was a little happier -which made classes more bearable. She had straightened things out with Noah, although he still had been etchy when she had gotten in a few good rides on Romana and Angela and she had gone off on their usual Tuesday ride. She was flattered by his surmising protectiveness.

But she kept predominately brooding over the anonymous, unknown horse. The movement in the trees had to of been him. She knew for a fact it wasn't just her imagination.

At lunch, Angela convened with Callie and the girls talked it up and laughed till the bell rang.

Callie made a stop at her locker when Andrew showed up as if he had been waiting for her to arrive at that precise moment.

"Hey Callie!" the jock greeted cheerily with too much animation.

"Oh, hey Andrew." She hoped this wouldn't start out as a bad habit he picked up; sneaking up on her every time she stopped at her locker. "How's it going?"

He sparked a grin. "Great! I'm really looking forward to next Friday."

"Yeah," said Callie at an attempt for the same level of enthusiasm. "Me too."

He stretched his ego smile even wider -if somehow it had been possible- at her response.

"I was thinking," he said, "that I could pick you up at your house at 6:30, since prom starts at 7:30 and all."

"Sounds perfect, Andrew. Thanks. I have to get to class." *Shouldn't you be there, too?* "I'll see you later." She offered him a smile so as not to come across as uninterested.

The guy was literally beaming as he made his way down the hall and into class. Callie sighed and kept her mother's words in her head for a friendly, uplifting reminder.

"Just stay positive," she murmured to herself.

All Callie wanted to do was get through the rest of her classes and bustle home to take Romana out on another ride. A good gallop. Especially since physically she could handle it no problem.

It took her seconds to gather her books and papers and zoom out the door. She plainly sped to her locker before Andrew could catch her again, slammed the locker closed with a little more force than necessary in her rush and paced extremely quickly to her bus. So fast in fact, that Callie had been the first one there. Which made her grow impatient just having to wait.

Slow pokes!

She was all revved up to get in the saddle.

Angela popped into view and came breezing past the seats to sit next to her best friend. She gave Callie a frown as she shuffled to get comfortable on this really hot day. The sun blazed down with its golden glow of radiating heat and hit Wyoming, full force unleashed.

"That's funny," teased Angela. "Usually you're one of the last ones on the bus. But today, you're the first..." She placed her index finger on her lip and looked up as if to think. "Hmm. Could it be because you're so desperately eager to ride Romana?"

Callie elbowed her in the ribs. "Ha ha."

Angie snickered. "Even if you were or not, we have to wait for the rest of the students," her friend pointed out.

"Not if I take over the bus and drive us home," said Callie as if the real idea appealed to her.

"That's just what you need," Angela joked. "Another car accident."

Callie flinched but her friend didn't notice. She knew Angela was just teasing and it wasn't meant seriously. But just the mention of an accident she couldn't even recall bothered her.

Then she thought of Noah. He had been uptight when she saw him this morning. Maybe he was just having a mood.

"Earth to Callie!"

Angela brought Callie back from her receded

contemplation and noticed her hand flashing back and forth in front of her face to grasp back her attention.

She shook her head out of her deep thoughts. "Sorry."

"What planet were you on, Mars?"

"No silly," said Callie, taking a turn at a joke. "Uranus, of course." The girls both laughed.

The bus finally started to file in with students and was soon on the road, wheeling for Callie's stop. Once there, she waved to Angela and hopped off, almost stumbling over her feet in her haste to see her mare ready and waiting at the pasture hill like always.

She walked the mile and the wooden sign labeled with their ranch's name touched her sight. Callie then picked up her feet into an excited jog towards the hill. Romana stood patiently grazing on the very top and abandoned her post the second she saw her sweet Callie climb over the fence.

Callie adjusted her backpack and swung over the mare's burnished and glossy bay back. She clutched mane and adapted into a comfortable sit.

Her horse's chocolate brown eyes twinkled.

Expectedly, Bailey and Panther materialized and the four raced for home. The wind hit Callie's face with a heavenly sensation of delight. It was a temporary shield from this Friday heat, which made her more excited.

It was the weekend and that always meant only one thing to Callie: more time for riding!

Callie slid on the bridle and buckled up the sheepskin girth, just as Noah emerged from around the tack room. He had noticed Romana's vacant saddle rack and bridle hook.

"Going for another ride?" he asked as if it hadn't been obvious enough.

"Sure am," came Callie's reply. Romana bobbed her head and snorted.

"Don't you think you should give the riding a little rest?"

Callie paused her tack-up process and stared at him like that had been the most absurd idea he had ever come up with.

"Why on earth would I do that?"

Noah shrugged to try and hide his feelings. There was something he wasn't telling Callie. She turned her entire body at him and pried him with a vigilant glare.

When he didn't answer, she prodded. "Noah, are you all right? You've seemed uptight in the last few days." Callie looked at him with concerned eyes. His were guarded.

He hid his face with his black Stetson. "Sure, I'm okay. As good as I can be."

She made a face. "What's that suppose to mean?"

Noah's mood started to show. "It just means that I can only ever be just *okay*, Callie." He tilted up his head again, staring at her hard. She knew exactly what he meant now.

"You're never going to let it go, are you?" she almost mumbled. It hadn't been intended to come out as a question.

"How can I? Things are never going to be the same, Callie. Never. And it's all my fault."

She couldn't believe he was blaming himself for the accident. An accident they had *both* suffered together.

"That accident was never your fault and you know it."

"Maybe you believe that," he jeered. "But I sure as hell don't. If I had been paying attention... If I had kept my eyes on the road..." He balled his hands into fists as he tried to finish. "I could have swerved out of the way. I could have saved you from all that pain. And you wouldn't have lost your memory."

Callie ground her teeth together.

"I could almost shoot myself for being so careless."

Her jaw dropped, horrified that those words ever rolled off his tongue.

"Noah Thomas Riley," Callie said slowly through gritted teeth. "You.Are.Not.To.Blame!" She made sure to emphasize each word carefully to get it through to his skull, her jaw set hard.

Romana stood quietly still as if to understand what was happening and didn't make a sound. Her ears scooped up her Callie's words to try and comprehend why she was upset so she could make it better. She easily sensed Callie was tense.

Callie continued. "If you want someone to blame, you can blame the man behind the wheel of that other car. I'm not the only one who suffered. You suffered, too, Noah. Not just me." *And the horse*, she supplemented to herself. "We suffered. But it's going to be okay."

"No, it's not!" refused Noah with hostility. "You can't remember me, Callie! You can't remember me!" Each time he said it was like a slap in the face. "How does that make it okay?!" he shouted.

Callie was speechless.

The horses all grew uneasy at his raised voice.

Hot tears blurred Callie's vision and obscured her thoughts.

She spun around and buried her face in Romana's mane. The mare curved her neck to try and console her sad, sad Callie.

Sorrow crept up stubbornly and thick in her throat and she swallowed hard to try and force it down.

I have to remember. I will remember, Noah. I promise you, I will remember.

Callie revealed her face again in time to turn around and see Noah vanish out of the barn.

It took Callie a really long time to settle down and collect her scattered thoughts and emotions. They were all muddled.

The trails stretched and set out in front of her and the only sounds she could hear were rustling leaves dancing from the wind, the rhythmic beat of Romana's hooves on the forkwood soil, the swaying of long grass blades and the chirping and singing of western meadowlarks that sat situated on boughs while they rambled past cottonwoods and sagebrush.

"I'm sure the only reason he blames himself is because that despicable driver isn't alive to take the blame for what he did," she muttered to her horse. Her situation was overwhelming.

How could Noah say such reckless and irrational things? He wouldn't need to shoot himself for being so 'careless'. Callie would shoot him herself for even thinking such a thing. It was ridiculous and it made no sense. She could not, would not, allow him to carry all this unnecessary weight on his shoulders.

Yes, Callie had been the one to lose her memory, but Noah had been there with her. That much she could remember. He had stuck with her and she didn't need her memory back to know that. She just did. There was closeness with Noah she could sense from the exterior of her skin to the very core of her inside.

Callie was going to find some way to prove it to him. But right now she felt detached from the world. Except for her mare, she felt alone.

Smoothly, Romana transitioned into a fluid trot down the path. Callie posted lightly and lost herself in the beat. 1 2, 1 2, 1 2, 1 2.

Until dinner time, she wouldn't even think about Noah. This time was for her. She'd release all preoccupying thoughts and just ride. Let her body and mind naturally flow with the horse and ride, nothing more.

Romana launched into a canter and Callie rocked with trancelike abstraction. 1 2 3, 1 2 3, 1 2 3.

As they hit the breach of open grassland, the sun

started to set on the bleak horizon. Horse and human became one even further and galloped full speed, head long against the wind.

This was what Callie was born to do. Speed might be a horse's secret weapon, but it was also the perfect way for Callie to escape, to fly.

Even if only for a while.

CHAPTER 11

C allie wriggled into her new prom dress.

In half hour, Andrew would come pulling up the driveway to pick her up. Butterflies fluttered and knots were tying themselves in her stomach.

All this past week she had busied herself with distracting duties to take her mind off Noah, but it was quite the challenge.

Everything's going to run great, she told herself. But the nerves wouldn't let her have it.

She fumbled with the zipper at the back but wasn't able to do it up all the way.

"Gah!" she flailed her arms out in frustration and let them limply crash against her thighs with a slap. She stared out the window at the horses for almost fifteen minutes, watching the horses play dominance games with each other.

There was three knocks on her door.

"Callie, sweetie?" came her mother's voice. "May I come in?"

Callie gave up on the stupid zipper. "Sure, mom. You can come in."

As the door pushed open, Lilly Marshall's head poked through first. When she saw Callie retry the stubborn thing one more time she smiled and came over to help. "Here, let me get that for you."

"Thanks."

"You look so beautiful, honey," said Lilly.

"Thanks," she said again, blushing a little. Then she sighed as a personal thought crossed her mind.

"Something on your mind?" Mom prompted, taking notice.

"It's Noah," Callie admitted. "He hasn't spoken a word to me since..." she paused.

"Since your argument?" finished her mother. Callie nodded slowly.

Lilly guided her daughter to the bed next to the window -and desk which was placed beside the book shelf packed with Callie's favorite books and country music- overlooking the horse pasture. She took a deep breath and hugged Callie's shoulders.

"You know he's just trying to look out for you, sweetie. This has been hard on him, too."

Callie latched on to what her mother was saying.

"I know that. But he thinks it's his fault, mom. That the accident could have been prevented if he had kept his eyes on the road."

"No one knows that for certain," said her mother.

"I sure don't," murmured Callie, downcast. "I don't remember the accident. He's so sure that me not remembering him is some sort of punishment for what happened." She looked at her mom despondently.

Lilly's grey eyes made warm contact with Callie that comforted her. Her mother would always be willing to listen and be there for her, no matter what. And she was glad to have that knowledge.

"Just try to understand what it was like for him to see you in pain, honey. What it did to him to see you in the hospital like that. What it was like for all of us. Sooner or later he'll learn to forgive himself, but it has to be on his own time."

Callie sighed heavily. "Okay, mom. I'll try."

"That's all I ask. Now," said Lilly assertively, standing up. "It's time to forget your problems and time to have fun at prom. Forget Noah for a while. Forget horses and just enjoy yourself, tonight," she grinned brightly.

Callie frowned at her mother.

"What?" Lilly asked, clueless.

Callie stared and waited.

"Oh," her mom laughed. "Right, asking you not to think about horses is like asking water not to be wet."

They both laughed.

A car honked outside their house.

"Well, that's my cue," said Callie.

Mother and daughter milled their way downstairs in time to catch David swinging open the door for Andrew

Dale. He stood tall in the door frame wearing a black three-button English style ultra high-twist wool tuxedo with a boutonniere and a collared shirt and tie matching Callie's green dress and traditional highly polished hard leather shoes with a curved toe to give a classic look.

The theme for their prom night was voted to be "New York City".

She decided to be simple and let her hair let loose with partial waves cascading down her back, wearing pretty black heels to match. Her wonderful mother had suggested that black went with everything. The dress was a sweetheart neckline with a corsage detail to the waist and black netted underskirt to hem with adjustable thin straps. A "masterpiece" on her as her father had put it. Then again, Dad was always looking to please and flatter his little Callie Bear.

Her father eyed her date up and down warily. He inspected him as if to find a reason to excuse Callie from being able to go.

"Hey Andrew, you look terrific." Callie came to stand at the doorway to the side with her parents. Mom had a black object in her hand. She tried to hide the horror she felt as she looked at the intimidating camera.

"Thanks Callie. You look very beautiful," said Andrew taking a step inside. The jock's hair was gelled into spikes and partially tousled.

"Here." He handed her a small silver box with a transparent lid that unveiled a pretty matching corsage for her.

Callie gratefully accepted, opened the box and

retrieved it, sliding it over her hand and resting it on her wrist. "Thanks. It's really pretty." She smiled up at him to let him know she really appreciated it. He beamed.

"Okay kids, time for a picture before you go!" hassled Lilly Marshall, camera ready for snapping.

Awkwardly, Callie and Andrew huddled in close together at the door smiling and posing, anticipating the flash. Andrew was too happy to slip his arm around her waist and hold it there till her mother was done.

Apparently this was only awkward for Callie.

As Lilly worked to adjust the settings and ready the flash, it was as if it had all been to taunt her mercilessly.

Take the picture already!

Her mom clicked the button, the flash set loose in their eyes and then it was done. Reluctantly, Andrew withdrew his arm.

It's just for one night, she reminded herself.

The two shuffled out the door, into the starry night and towards Andrew's silver jeep.

Andrew quickly settled into the driver's seat and waited for Callie to find her way to the passenger's side.

Gee, what a gentleman, she thought sarcastically. She took her seat, secured her belt -which her date thought he was too good for- and rolled down her window to snatch some fresh air.

Within seconds, the key rotated in the ignition and they were on the rode, ready for "New York City".

The music blared loudly in Callie's ears as her and her date strolled in together right after taking their picture at the door.

The prom committee had outdone themselves and Powder River High School's gym looked spectacular. It truly was a taste of New York City in Natrona County.

The bodies swaying on the dance floor moved energetically to the music. The music's beat rumbled under their feet and stimulated their eardrums.

Callie mingled for a while all the way to the punch table -Andrew disappeared into the bathroom- in which was surrounded by appetizing platters. She was anything but hungry and was happy to pour herself a small cup of the red drink.

While taking her time to sip from the small plastic cup, Callie spotted Mark and Tyler go into the men's restroom, which was also a boy's change room. She recognized them as two of Andrew's friends who were also on the football team with him.

Callie squinted her eyes to try and make out what the two players were carrying in their arms, but what ever it had been, their team jackets were covering it. Her stomach churned. Maybe her date had ditched her.

He can take all night if that's what he'd rather do. She rolled her eyes and stuck to the gymnasium's wall while the time passed and the music continued.

Unexpectedly, a song that reminded her of Noah began to play and she grimaced. She couldn't allow herself to think of him. This was her prom night.

Half hour must have passed and Callie grew irritated. Andrew had asked her to prom for what exactly? To dump her at the entrance and spend his time in the men's room?

I should just call home.

Just as the thought presented itself, Andrew and his two friends, Mark and Tyler, came out of the change room. Oh well, she had better things to do than to stick around with the narcissistic jock.

She fished out her phone from her hand purse and dialed home; she hoped someone was in the house.

Suddenly, Angela appeared, waving excitedly to her best pal who she evidently was glad to of found.

The phone rang four times.

With a change of plans, Callie hung up.

Angela cut across the crowd and walked over. At the same time, Andrew seemed to of been searching the large group of students for his date.

Ex-date, she corrected herself. It was fine; she had her best friend to keep her company now. Andrew could go drown in the punch for all she cared.

"Callie! You look great!" said Angie with a dynamic friendly smile.

"You too, Angie!" Callie told her as she scanned that her friend wore her hair up in an elegant bun, dangly earrings, white heels and a dazzling blue dress that dropped just above her knees. "What a night!" she exclaimed.

"Where's your date?" Angie peered around and to Callie's left and right.

Callie didn't reply. She would rather Angela solved it for herself so she could skip having to explain the gruesome details. Wherever Andrew *Jerk* Dale was right now didn't concern her.

Angela understood immediately. "Ohhh," was her genius response. "Um, you want to go get some fresh air?"

Callie nodded, taking up the offer. "Sure let's go." With good timing, too, because the second the words left her mouth, Andrew's search came to an end and he seemed to be staggering her way clumsily.

The girls passed a number of babbling students before reaching the doors and stepping out.

"So he just ditched you?" asked Angela as the music got muffled by the outer school walls.

"Yup, you were right, Angie. I should have listened."

Angela shrugged, forgiving her without second thought. "Boys will be boys."

Not all boys, thought Callie. There was one she could think of that outclassed guys like Jerk Dale any day. But she kept the thought to herself.

Suddenly, Andrew barged through the doors and stumbled down the steps. It took all of his effort not to fall. Out behind him followed his little possy.

"Hey Callie! I've been lookin' everywhere for ya!" he said too loudly. Mark and Tyler laughed like it was the funniest thing they ever heard. But it didn't take a rocket scientist to figure out that they were all drunk.

As he neared closer to her, she could practically smell the vile reeking alcohol, stenching up her nose.

The five of them were all alone in the parking lot and Callie instantly grew nervous.

Angela stayed close to her. They both smelled more than just the alcohol. They smelled trouble.

"Sorry I took so long," he spluttered stupidly. He swung his arm around her shoulders and she flinched, struggling to get loose. Mark and Tyler burst out in a new set of guffaws.

Poor Angela stood frozen in place, pale as a sheet.

Andrew's free hand clasped Callie's chin and he leaned in and gave her a forceful kiss. His hold tightened around her and she went into defensive mode. Desperately, she tried to squirm out of his iron grip.

"Awe, c'mon! Don't be like that!" Andrew complained. His breath was repulsive.

"Let go of me!" she cried scathingly.

Callie didn't realize a car sped up down the lot. She pushed against the tall jock's chest to no avail. She kicked and shoved until Mark and Tyler started to pull her into them and push her around. She heard a vehicle screech to a halt and a door slam closed.

Andrew reclaimed his hold on her again and she was thrown to the ground. Her hands and knees abraded against the cement.

Callie rolled on her back in time to see a solitary figure in the night time darkness come out of nowhere and lunge fist first at Andrew's face. The startled football player fell to the ground with a hard thud and scrambled to get to his feet.

Before the jock had time to fully straighten, the figure -who Callie realized with provided lucent lighting, was Noah- rammed against him and angrily unleashed another blow to the jaw and then to the nose. Blood spewed down and dripped to the pavement.

Mark and Tyler dumbly charged at him but a furious, raging Noah easily struck them with nasty hits to the gut. They ran out of sight into the blackness and Callie felt a sob choke her.

She shouldn't have stood there so helpless and defenseless. To be powerless against them had relentlessly hurt her, even with the relief that pulsated within her of Noah liberating her.

Andrew didn't give in so easily. His pride had other ideas. So as Callie allowed her emotions run her now she jumped to her feet, refused to look at Angela and ran as fast as she could, through the parking lot, across the empty silent road and far into the trees that covered her. She didn't stop. Instead, she just kept going till she couldn't anymore. All she knew at this point in time was that she was capable of running for a long distance. She wouldn't stop till her lungs begged her to. She ran and ran, painfully deeper into the shadows of the woods, tripping every few minutes. Deeper into the dense wilderness that consumed her.

CHAPTER 12

Callie shambled unthinkingly through the woods. She didn't want to say it out loud -afraid of breaking what was left of her sanity and crying to no end- but she was lost.

The darkness barely permitted her already adjusted eyes to see anything. Despite it all -being exhausted, feeling confused and detached from the world, prom going all wrong, the rest of her memory obstinately hiding from her- she kept going. If she kept going, maybe it wouldn't feel like she was giving up. If she stopped, it would make her fall apart because she did not even know what to do with herself anymore. So she kept walking for the sake of having reason, not because she wanted to run away.

Was she, though? Running away? It didn't feel like running away exactly. It felt like she wanted to find answers.

A number of blind trips to the dirt had ruined her

dress. Callie glowered into the darkness as the memory of Andrew evilly threaded in her head. The image of Noah's fist being hurled to disproportion his sorry face made her feel a little better, though.

Serves him right!

Her attention kept swerving like a misdirected arrow. She wanted to target what really mattered. Recovering the rest of the memory she had lost and just focus on horses for the rest of her life. It just had to be one step at a time.

Now a question hung in her mind that itched to be answered. How had Noah been able to show up with such impeccable timing the way he did?

Her first guess was he had been spying on her; keeping an eye on her for whatever reason which belonged to him. Her second guess was someone had spilled that Andrew Dale had been her date to prom and he disliked that idea so much, enough to come down and check to see if he approved.

But why would he care?

Angela had been straightforward about telling Callie Andrew couldn't be trusted. That before Callie had lost her valuable memory, she didn't like Mr. Self-centered. In conclusion, Angela had been right. She was able to fully acknowledge that now.

Working to piece her scattered thoughts, she faintly heard scrunching within the bushes and undergrowth. Her foot falls became more wary and mindful.

Howling and yipping broke through the brisk night silence.

Uneven breathing was the only sound that she made. Something about the way the atmosphere sensed to her unsettled Callie and her uneasiness took effort to properly contain.

There it was again; but this time she was quiet enough to make out the rumbling of an angry growl in an animal's chest.

Callie's body froze solid. Her veins turned to ice. In that instant, she knew she wasn't alone.

Romana stirred restlessly and circled in her stall. The mare's hooves pawed at her straw bedding and whinnied and snorted. The rest of the horses picked up on her anxiety and soon enough mimicked her example of distress.

Her Callie was in trouble and she had to go to her. Her nostrils flared impatiently, she shook her head and with a swish of her tail she neighed loudly with it echoing down the aisle and out the barn doors.

Next, she did something she knew she wasn't allowed to do; she kicked her stall door. The dark, blood bay didn't have to keep at it for long. Adrian came plodding in to snare the culprit that the commotion belonged to.

"Romana," said the ranch hand displeased. "What's gotten into you?"

Headlights flashed past for about two seconds and then when Adrian's attention vacillated away from her she resumed her desperate kicks.

He sharply turned his head and unbolted the latch,

opening it till it had a wide enough gap of space for her to squeeze past a dumbfounded Adrian and raced towards the trails.

Noah came sprinting into the barn, Angela right behind.

"What happened?!" he panted. "And where's Lilly and David?"

"I'll explain later. We've got to catch that mare!" Adrian hollered.

"The mare can wait, Adrian," said Noah seriously, putting out his hand to stop him.

"What in the world for?" the 31-year old asked bewildered, exchanging glances at Noah, to Angela and back to Noah.

Noah eyed him hard, his mouth a tight line before responding. "Callie's gone missing."

⟿—⟿—⟿

Romana flawlessly pounded down the trails.

Her bonding instincts that connected her to the human she loved dearly reeled her in from one direction to the next. The mare slowed to a trot and dipped her head to try and draw in a familiar scent.

Nothing.

Intuition was just going to have to drive her to Callie. Until miles from Silver Creek, Romana's muzzle vibrated as she sniffed in the smell of something familiar. Or rather, *someone* familiar. She had been here. Her Callie had been here. She could recognize it anywhere.

Hastily, she traced Callie's path and initiated a gallop, dashing with incredible speed past the blurring silhouettes of trees. There was no dirt path here. Callie had strayed without direction. She fled into this wilderness where she had to be found.

With soft earth under her powerful hooves, Romana drew in the scent of something else. A smell she didn't trust. It got mixed in with the scent of her human.

And just like that, she kicked into a new flight of speed.

"He what?!" roared David Marshall. "Andrew Dale did what to my daughter?!" The corners of his mouth were practically foaming. "When I get my hands on him..."

They all hurried to tack up horses –Noah on Black Bear, Darla and Bandit, Lilly and Mocha, Adrian and Trigger, and David on Denver- to set out on a search. Darla, more than willingly, had joined them.

"Calm down, David," ordered Lilly to her fuming husband. "We need to concentrate on finding Callie right now. And it appears Noah beat you to the punch... Literally."

"I'm really sorry Mrs. Marshall," Noah said remorsefully, tightening Bear's cinch.

After Adrian and Noah's stories were exposed, the main number one factor was to find Callie.

"I know I don't approve of violence to solve anything, but just this once, I'll gladly let it slide," Lilly said darkly through furious tight lips. "But we need to focus on Callie," she reminded firmly.

"I'm betting that's exactly where Romana went," Darla said without doubt in her voice.

Adrian nodded at his wife, agreeing with her assumption.

"I just don't understand why she ran," said Noah still trying to force it to make sense.

"She's lost most of her memory," Adrian pointed out. "She's just trying to put her life back together. And she's been through a heck of a lot. It must have been too overwhelming for her. So she did the only thing she thought was right."

They all stared at him.

"She fled away from the pain and confusion. From what scared her. Like a horse would do. Flee from pain, danger, or anything that scared it. She's *scared*," he simplified.

Tears welled in Lilly's eyes at hearing the words being spoken. David consoled her with a hug.

Noah ground his teeth determinedly.

"We're going to find her," he told them with defiant certainty. "So help me God, we're going to find her."

CHAPTER 13

Twisting slowly around, ferocious sharp teeth -too sharp for her liking- threatened Callie.

The wild coyote's yellow eyes vigorously held her in place. She was paralyzed and couldn't move.

Think Callie, think! She could scream at it, she could pelt rocks, but should she really risk angering the vehement canine even more?

No, wait!

She backpedalled to what her father had taught her when she was only a little girl about encountering a coyote.

Raise your arms up in the air to make yourself look bigger. Make loud noises by yelling or banging things together... She'd have to yell. Back away slowly from the coyote if it doesn't run away. And if the coyote attacked -which she dreadfully tried not to think it would come to that- she would have to fight back.

Great, she remembered. But what good would it do her if she couldn't even get her nervous system to co-operate?

Usually when coyotes learned if humans weren't a danger to them they would be very brazen. Which meant if this female coyote was acting this way, there was something she was protecting that Callie got too close for the animal's liking; offspring, perhaps, or strictly territorial claim?

She concealed a scream and was doused with fear. There would be no way she could outrun the undomesticated dog. You were never supposed to turn your back on them or run away. That was just asking for it. Callie knew that game would already be lost before it even begun.

Callie tested one of her options: backing away slowly. But as she stepped backward progressively, she bumped against a fallen tree trunk that ensnared her. She bit her lip, panicked, and with severe rigid shoulders stifled the loud shriek that pleaded to be let ripped out from her throat.

Her options of tactic still remained opened for use but Callie's eyes only held vacancy in the darkness.

It must have been her adrenaline talking, but suddenly she straightened up, taller, and gave the rough-coated dog a hard mean stare and began shouting, raising her arms up in the air. "Get! Go on, get out of here!"

The monstrously large female coyote faltered back no steps and didn't even track any forward. Her teeth stayed bared and menacing, and even curled up over her teeth a little more.

A piercing neigh travelled through the night, bouncing off the trees. Even in the nocturnal darkness that didn't let Callie see as well during the day, she peripherally descried lightning fast hooves pulsing in the distance, enclosing the void quickly enough and -in the available open space of the cottonwood stalk- the horse released herself over it like a coil, sailing, and then landing with inches to spare on the other side in front of Callie.

She planted herself protectively in front of her timid, frantic human. Ears back so flat, they were hidden.

Any horse in their right mind would flee from such a circumstance. They would take flight and let their survival instincts take over. But Callie's horse came to her rescue and she wasn't going to budge.

She watchfully measured how her mare reacted to the coyote that stood in close proximity to her and Callie.

Callie knew that once a horse felt cornered, she would likely put up a fight. Romana was ready to do anything possible. It was like a wild mare protecting her defenseless foal.

Which was what this defensive female coyote was doing: protecting her own vulnerable young near by.

Twice in one night Callie had felt defenseless but she couldn't afford to let her focus get sidetracked right now. *Especially* right now.

Callie was shocked and surprised. This was the first time she had ever seen her horse so dangerously aggressive.

Romana's eyes were as cold as ice. Her tendons and

bunched muscles bulged out as she pawed at the dirt and angrily switched her tail. She snorted and flared her nostrils in direct warning.

The feral canine sidestepped to try and get closer, but Romana only yielded her haunches slightly, refusing to let her forequarters be pressured away. And then she began pawing at the earth once more. Her dominance was escalating and the determined mare would not back down.

The dog snarled and barked rebelliously.

At that, Romana half-reared and Callie was ready to pick up stones and begin tossing them at the animal. Her mare was willing to defend her, so Callie was ready to also fight for her dear horse.

For a split second she pondered at how she had been capable of escaping her stall. By now her family would be searching for her.

Callie's horrorstruck expression remained tight.

Romana decided she had had enough and fully reared up towards the sky, her hooves deathly lethal weapons, coming back down and rapidly lunging at the startled dog with sharp razor teeth of her own. Her warning had not caused the wild coyote to flee so she would have to make her.

The intractable female backed away to avoid getting trampled but attempted to hold her ground.

Romana flicked her tail in enormous irritation and reared again, releasing a high pitched squeal that caused the feral dog to retrieve a few more steps. To this, the angry horse knew she was winning. The enemy was yielding to her prevailing pressure -not the other way round. Her flattened ears stayed hidden and she continued to work on driving them away.

Callie worked on exuding composure rather than panic. If she panicked, it would tear away her ability to think.

With her mare encroaching more and more on the predator's berth, she unsealed another high pitched neigh and towered over the now shrinking dog with one final persistent rear that made the coyote finally give in and dart into the night, vanishing.

In realization that she had been holding her breath, Callie huffed out in huge relief. Romana's ears flitted back in her direction and bent her pretty head to stare at her now-safe human.

Wet hot tears rolled down Callie's face and she shakily stumbled with open arms to encase her hero in a tight hug. She began sobbing in the mare's black silky mane, wrapping her weak, jelly arms on her satiny neck and her horse stood patiently, comforting her Callie with long awaited security.

They were safe now.

"Okay, girl," said Callie, bleakly, still a little precarious. "Take us home."

Callie's feet were sore from her black heels so she had slipped them off and tiredly sat on Romana's velvet back.

Her dress had been ruined and frayed. To make it easier on herself she split it up her thigh partially so she was actually able to ride a little more comfortably.

She couldn't stop thanking her beautiful horse for saving her life.

Whilst Callie clamped to the mare's long, soft mane, she moved as the horse moved, her powerful legs worked over backtracking towards their home. Silver Creek would soon be in reachable range and that's where Callie would take a hot shower, change into warm pajamas, crawl into bed under her horse covers and cuddle with her lovable Labradors.

Callie could never imagine Bailey and Panther as vicious as the wild dog she had encountered, but soon realized if the ones they loved were in danger, they were more than capable of hounding on anyone who meant to bring harm.

Romana could vividly see through the starlit night; she guided them on to a dirt trail that Callie instantly recognized.

And she would have galloped for home except she was too worn out to grip around her horse's belly afraid that they'd probably cause her to drift to the side and fall off.

Plus, Romana's walk methodically calmed and soothed Callie. A rhythm she'd never get tired of.

"It was stupid of me to of run away," Callie was talking to her equine friend now that she felt more relaxed and at ease. She was settled down enough to speak.

Romana's ears filled up with her partner's words, intently listening.

"I was so afraid, girl," she continued. "I ran because I

didn't know what to do with myself. You and Noah have both saved me tonight. I don't know what I would have done without you two." Callie leaned forward and tightly hugged the horse -full of fidelity- in heart-felt sincerity. "You're going to get a well earned bucket full of my home-made horsey treats. You were so brave!"

Romana bobbed her head up and down as if to say: *Well, if you're offering, who am I to turn you down?*

Riding past the thicket of shadowed trees, the pit of Callie's stomach twisted. She sat bolt upright on Romana's bare back and skimmed what surrounded them. Edginess was chafing raw against her intuitive instincts. Her heart thudded unevenly. Even Romana's eyes, Callie could sense, were riveted distantly into the forest and no longer fixated on the route ahead. Her rhythmic hoof beats slowed and then halted.

Jointly, they didn't stir. Romana started to get nervously keyed up and now it had transferred into Callie.

Fear revisited them and they held statuesquely right in the middle of the trail.

The unwanted feeling that danger was lurking where they could not see it was messing with Callie's head.

This is such a marvelous night, Callie couldn't help to think sarcastically.

"Oh!"

Callie grasped a set of yellow eyes suddenly pinning her in a shocked state.

Romana was taken by surprise and threw her head back.

"Callie!" came a frantic, anxious cry from a remote direction. The voice that called her name ricocheted off the cottonwoods.

She had been right. Someone had been searching for her. Or rather, more than someone.

Callie imprisoned her voice. The vicious dog must have felt her territory still being threatened. She was now issuing a warning display at the two intruders.

"Callie! Where are you?!"

It sounded like Noah! Callie wanted to bellow out his name but the blood had drained from her face and her lips trembled. She flexed her brain for any bright ideas to escape.

Hadn't this coyote had enough from the last time?

Was it just Callie, or was she oddly attracting one disaster after the other tonight?

If she had known the raiding predicaments that had been awaiting her, she would have barricaded herself in her room and wouldn't come out till it hit a new day. But it already was. It was no longer Friday. It was Saturday; Callie just didn't know what time it was -as if she had lost track of everything; her thoughts, her memories, her feelings. It had all gone missing and to find it made her feel hopeless.

She was so close to exploding. Every minute she neared closer to the countdown of an internal bomb, ready to detonate.

"Callie! Can you hear me, Callie?!"

Yes! Yes, Noah, I can hear you!

The coyote lost all patience and lunged at Romana's forelegs, but then made an attempt to pounce on her haunches. She reared, and Callie fought to stay on.

With the calming beats of her horse's momentum, she had been half asleep. But wide awake now. It felt like she was living through a nightmare. Except, it was really happening.

She afforded a second to guess that Noah and Bear were strategically coordinating themselves to find her.

Horses could see so well in the night time, that with Black Bear's and Romana's perceptivity, they would never have a problem to find their way. So while Callie uncontrollably anticipated Noah to ride to her rescue -again- she wondered if he would get there on time.

But there was no more time. The furry figure reproached with another attack and baring sharp teeth that this time, when Romana reared to avoid getting bitten, Callie's imprisoned voice was set free and she screamed. Her legs failed their hold around the frightened mare's barrel and she tipped backward, landing in the dirt with a harsh smack.

Her head collided with the ground and Callie's world went dark.

CHAPTER 14

⊸—⊸—⊸—⊸—⊸—⊸—⊸—⊸—⊸—⊸—⊸—⊸—

U nder tiers of Callie's oblivion, she saw a free spirited galloping horse coming towards her. His eyes were glazed with delicate pride and majestic power. His mane flowed like a river, streaming silkily amidst his brawny neck. His wonderfully-shaped head exemplified intelligence and warmth like the sun. His coasting advance was like an eagle soaring on air. A ghostly angel coming to her. He exempted a melodic neigh which stunned her. The most beautiful sound.

Her psyche began to alternate and the ghostly creature faded. *Wait... Don't go...* She thought.

The heavy darkness that pushed down on her became lighter and raised her closer to consciousness.

The first thing Callie was aware of -besides her bashing headache that thrummed like a violent earthquake- was a soft firm hand brushing along her forehead and through her hair. They were gentle strokes, but yet anxious at the same time.

She lifted her eyelids and saw stars up above of the blanketed night sky past the gaps of the trees bordering the trail.

"Callie?" came Noah's relieved voice when he saw her open her eyes. His well defined, angular face was inches from hers. She smelt his wonderful breath on her tongue almost.

Something was different to Callie, though. Not entirely different, but not quite the same, either.

"Callie," Noah's prompting handsome voice said again. "Can you hear me? Please say something," he pleaded in a low eager tone. His expression was intense.

A swell of overwhelming emotion crashed on her with a wave of urgency.

Flashing vivid images played in her head, coming on so unexpectedly: talking to Noah on the way back from town, Noah prying Callie's eyes in confusion, the unsteady Chevvy wheeling ruthlessly fast at them on the wrong side of the road, the clash of shattering glass, a terrified horse fighting all of his worth to escape his cage.

I remember everything! It's unbelievable!

Callie blinked rapidly, surprised by the splurges of memoirs.

Noah's eyebrows stressfully pulled together over his concerned eyes. "Callie. I'm going insane. Please say something! Talk to me. Anything!"

His frantic hysteria pleased Callie, because that's one more thing she gladly recollected: she was in love with

Noah Riley. And here he was, hovering over her. He had rescued her.

The wild dog was nowhere to be seen. It was absolutely silent.

Despite Callie's harbored feelings for Noah -never willing to admit to him that she more than just wanted to be friends- she propped herself up, ignoring her pounding headache, she contorted her waist to face him, stared deep into his startled hazel eyes and kissed him fiercely.

Whether she was thinking or wasn't thinking at all made absolutely no difference to Callie. She closed her eyes and morphed her lips to his and realized he was suddenly kissing her back. His fingers gripped her from behind, shoving her closer into him while she curled her fingers into his jet black hair and refused to allow anything but the pleasant bliss that surged through her interrupt.

No words, just kissing.

Black Bear and Romana silently stood to the side of the path, snatching at grass. The two horses had performed remarkably tonight.

Noah was the first to regain control, disentangling himself reluctantly from Callie.

Callie took more effort to regenerate composure but managed it, as well. They both panted so loudly it was almost embarrassing.

"Callie..." Noah shook his head, questions filling his glazed eyes on hers, absolutely bewildered. "What was *that?*" He sounded amazed. "How hard did you hit your head, exactly?"

Before responding, Callie took a deep breath. "I remember..." she whispered happily.

"You what?" his voice raised in astonishment.

"I remember everything Noah! I remember!" Her voice rose in emphasized jubilation.

Callie was a mess, with her torn dress, dirty bare feet and mangled hair, but she shimmered with exhilaration. Noah was experiencing his own exuberance. He didn't care the condition that her appearance was in. She would always be beautiful to him; his Callie, always.

Best of all, Callie had remembered everything. And she had kissed him! If he could, he would have shouted it over the mountain tops.

"I can't believe it!" he exclaimed. But then with an exhaling huff of relief, he made a face at her. "I was so worried about you. Don't you ever do that to me again, Callie." His voice was too light to be angry. It felt like an onerous weight had been lifted right off his shoulders.

Callie was about to throw a million apologies at him. "Noah, I'm so sorry. I..."

He cut her off by occupying her lips, keeping them too busy to talk. When he finally surfaced, he said "You don't need to apologize, Callie. I'm the one who should be apologizing."

"I'm ready to debate you on that one," she diverged with a mumble.

"How do you feel?" he asked her gently, taking her in his arms and resting her head on his chest.

"I have the world's worst headache," she qualified.

"I could make it better," he offered with a smug grin tugging at his lips.

A smile played on the edges of Callie's lips as well, but she exercised restraint.

"Very tempting," she unwillingly resisted, "but I'll take a rain check. Besides, it's dying down. And we should get back. Everyone, I assume, is still searching for me."

"Mmm," Noah replied thoughtfully.

"Oh, one more thing," said Callie as Noah slowly helped her to her feet.

"Yes?"

"I never did thank you for saving me."

He laughed, his hand holding hers. "From your prom date or an infuriated wild dog?"

Callie made a sour face just having to think of it. "Both," she finally said. "I should have never agreed to go with him."

"No, you shouldn't have," he easily granted. "But everything's okay, now. May I ask you something, though?"

Noah put his eyes on her, waiting.

She hesitated at first, but said "Sure."

"What were you thinking about, that day of the... accident? You looked like you really wanted to ask me something. I'm just curious..."

Callie turned her head to stare at Romana as she thought. The mare felt her human's eyes resting on her and paused from grazing to return a glance in her direction.

She had wanted to ask Noah how his father had been

doing. She had refrained from asking him, knowing perfectly well it was a touchy subject. Noah had a tough time dealing with an alcoholic for a father enough as it was without needing people like her to remind him.

Much less ask how he was getting through it. Provided she only had good hearted intentions because she cared about him. A lot.

Noah brought her wandering thoughts back. "You know you can tell me anything, don't you?" he murmured.

"Yes," she mumbled. But there had been plentiful hardship for one night. She'd confront him another day. Under better circumstances.

"Another time?" he practically read her mind.

Callie only nodded.

"Okay." He swept her cheek with the back of his russet skinned hand. Her eyes drifted back to his alluring face. She was herself at last. In the end she had gained more than she'd lost.

Noah's comforting expression held her. "Let's get you home."

He mounted Bear and assisted Callie in sitting behind him. She warped her arms around his waist and buried her face in his back, inhaling his brilliant essence.

Romana happily followed closely behind.

CHAPTER 15

O n account of Callie's return, everyone had been truly relieved that she had been found and back at home.

Lilly and David Marshall had gotten too worked up about her being safely in their hugging arms that they had skipped any lectures they had been internally practicing -deciding she had been through enough.

Callie had slept and ate well, now treading along her favorite trail in an atmosphere of solitude. Just her and Romana, trotting right on past Lester Lake on a clear blue day with not a cloud in existence. Which is how her head felt: clear. It was a really good feeling.

It gave Callie even more room to mentally picture the beautiful, ghostly horse in her head. It was hard to convince herself he was real. The way she felt when she thought about the amazing dreamy four-legged creature provoked her to want to find him just that much more badly.

When she re-gathered the image of him gracefully sailing to her in her unconscious state, the memory forced a beckoning impulse to feed that want more severely. To grow at an indescribable rate.

In fact, if she hadn't known any better, she would committally gamble that the mysterious missing horse had been calling to her. The memory of his lovely dazzling neigh sent a rocketing, thrilling rush in her veins.

Numerous sentiment thoughts were percolating in Callie's head.

The baffling enigmatic horse that was only a fantasy to her swarmed her devotion to discovering him, and it set her up for failure and disappointment, but she was keenly prepared for that risk.

A penetrating yelp shrilled above them.

She lifted her eyes to the sky in time to see a magnificent sight that perplexed her. There, soaring, in an incredible aerial display of freedom and power, was a golden eagle. His wings expanded away from his body, allowing the air to carry him. She was struck with awe.

As the pair dwindled now into the cover of the trees, birds greeting them with welcoming chirps, Callie deviated Romana towards Indian Creek. It was a slim, narrow hope, but a hope she still clung to regardless.

"Faint chance he'll be here, girl. But we can at least try," she told the sauntering mare.

Her hands became very taut around the braided leather reins. The water course came into view a while later and surged calmly, reflecting a glistening, expanding streak of yellow sunlight that travelled down for miles.

"I wonder what his story is," she brooded, stopping at the fringe of the creek. She dismounted and stood in the grass for a few minutes, musing.

The eagle remained circling overhead, like he was watching them with some sort of interest.

The quietness that Callie eased into as she stared into the water, watching her reflection, transposed and her ears -as well as Romana's- captured a subdued sound on the other side of the snaking brook.

Her heart missed a beat and she didn't move, craving to incline her head.

Her chest rose with her unsteady breathing. Without so much as an indicative warning -like whatever had remained curtained behind the shadowed outlines of the trees- now lithely manifested before her as a mirrored, rippling mirage in the water, and she mindfully carried her bright green eyes to where she had to stifle an awestruck gasp.

He had come.

The compulsion was too dire, and she caved in, slowly looking up.

Callie's stomach flipped with devastating joy at what she detained sight of.

The stallion was more enchanting than she had ever dared to imagine. It mesmerized her.

He stood stanced as a proud Dun Blanket Appaloosa Mustang stallion. By his musculature definition, she knew he had incredible speed, endurance and sure-footedness.

His golden dun color radiated in the fiery sunset and a white, spotted blanket on his flanks. A coal black mane and tail with black stockings on his powerful legs, dark chocolate brown eyes that glinted with the same majestic magic she had remembered. His all-round, perfectly conformed face held more intelligence than she had credited. In between those two hypnotic eyes ran a snowy blaze marking down to his sensitive flaring nostrils which enticed her.

This horse extracted a far better realism in resemblance to her dreams.

He was real.

The free-roaming beauty had been unscathed and was gloriously unharmed.

Romana whinnied a curious hello and broke into her deep, submerged trance.

Callie's hand burned to stretch out her arm and reach to touch this inexplicable, bodily gift. Her fingers twitched with yen.

The stallion insightfully studied her. Their eyes locked and the fighting impulse won over as Callie absently stretched out her hand reflexively. Like looking into the window through his mind, losing herself in his eyes had set it off naturally.

But the fascinating creature gracefully resilienced from her and whirled away, his willowy momentous frame dancing and evaporated out of view.

When Callie looked up, the eagle, too, had departed.

Her heart fell to the floor as he vanished, but she could

not override the victorious happiness she was experiencing. It made her uncharacteristically hyper.

A frenzy had begun for Callie Marshall. It was not the last time she would see the horse of setting suns, whose coat emanated like the golden orb in the endless skies. The stallion was gone for now. But she would reunite with the boundless mustang once again.